COCKER AND I

A Novel

ANTHONY MCDONALD

Anchor Mill Publishing

Cocker and I

Anchor Mill Publishing
4/04 Anchor Mill
Paisley PA1 1JR
SCOTLAND
anchormillpublishing@gmail.com

Artwork on cover: Copyright Lopolo. © Shutterstock. 'Sexual life - gay couple on the bed'.The individuals depicted in this artwork are models. No inference in regard to their sexual orientation may be drawn from the content of the book.

Anthony McDonald

For John and Bryan

Cocker and I

ONE

My room-mate's name was Cocker. And it wasn't even his second name. It was his first. It was written on the door when I arrived. Cocker Davis. He'd got here before me, written his name up, dumped his kit on his bed and gone out. There was only a small card for us to write our two names on. He'd used most of the space for his. I had to write my name smaller and underneath. Pip Rogers. OK. That's funny too, if you insist. Depends on the context. It would have been funnier if I'd put my name up first.

I hadn't really expected to have a room-mate. Most first-year students had single rooms. There were just a few who'd have to share. I'd read about this, but assumed I wouldn't be one of them. I was wrong about that.

There's something not all that nice about waiting for someone to turn up when that someone has already been in your bedroom – which is also his bedroom – and made his mark on it. I had no way of knowing what to expect. I'd been to boarding school, and was used to dormitories and, later, shared rooms in my last years. But then I'd always known the people I was sharing with. I wasn't used to sharing my living space with complete strangers.

As I unpacked my stuff and stuffed it into drawers and cupboards my imagination came up with increasingly negative images of what this guy Cocker would be like.

He might be massive (I was quite petite) and insensitive. He might be a nerd, with a more than unpleasant amount of acne. He might be a total dick. Actually, with a name like his he probably was.

And then the door opened suddenly and in he walked.

My heart stopped. At least it felt as if it did. I wasn't supposed to find boys beautiful... Men, sorry. At university we were supposed to call ourselves men, not boys... I wasn't supposed to find members of my own sex beautiful ... but I did.

He was fractionally taller than me and just a little bit better developed in terms of muscle. His hair was thick and dark brown. Blue eyes shone out of a lovely, frankly smiling face. He said, 'Hi, Pip,' walked up to me and we shook hands.

'Hi, Cocker,' I said. 'Saw your name on the door.'

'Sorry I wrote it a bit big. Didn't leave much room for yours. Wasn't thinking.'

'No worries,' I said. 'Plenty room for both.'

'Just as well you didn't get here first, though,' Cocker said.

'Why?' I asked, feeling a frown pinching my forehead.

'Pip rogers Cocker Davis? C'mon!' His smile curled up wickedly, and we shared our first laugh.

He had gone out to buy milk, sugar and tea. I had just put a packet of biscuits in my sock drawer. There was a kettle. Cocker made us tea and I got the biscuits out from among the socks. It was five o'clock. An October evening. Shortly there would be a welcome meeting. Then dinner in hall... Freshers' Week was about to kick off. I felt Cocker and I had made a good start.

A whirl of new names, new faces, those of boys and girls. All a bit daunting. I wasn't used to girls. Boarding school boy, me, and I lived in remote countryside at home. After dinner six of us, all from the same staircase, decided to head out and find a pub. We were men, the six of us, and that was what men did. I'd just turned eighteen and much the same went for the rest of us.

One of the guys, who was called Richard, said, Let's go to the Lamb and Flag. It was only a short walk. Past The Randolph Hotel and left into St Giles. The Randolph would have a bar, of course, but it looked a bit posh for a first tentative outing by the likes of us. More the sort of place we'd book our parents into when they came up to visit, perhaps.

We'd been deluged with information. About our college. About the university. Clubs and societies we could join... We talked about those now. Richard wanted to get onto a hockey team. Another guy said rowing was his big thing. One of his main reasons for wanting to come to Oxford. I piped up and said I wanted to join one of the drama groups.

I was rather a shy boy, actually, but I'd found at school that acting roles in plays went some way to dealing with this. 'There's a production of Hamlet,' I said. 'I wouldn't mind getting a part in that.'

'You'll be lucky,' said one of the others. 'Competition's fierce.'

I shrugged. 'You can only try,' I said.

I drank a pint of bitter with the others. Then I had a second one. I'd rarely done that. But here I was, embarking on a new life. We all had a third one. Bit of a voyage of discovery, that. At least I wasn't the only one of us to stagger occasionally on the way back. And we did find the right college, and the right staircase. And none of us threw up.

I'd worried a little about getting undressed in front of Cocker. I was a bit shy, as I've said. There are some blokes who just get their kit off in front of anyone, without being remotely bashful about it. I've noticed they tend to be the guys with the biggest balls and dicks.

I'm not a very big bloke in any department. Unlike in the case of some smallish guys my cock is not a startling exception to that. It's perfectly in proportion to the rest of me. I'm not ashamed of it. Even so, that was one of the reasons I gave a thought to how I'd deal with bedtime with my new room-mate. Probably we'd both do it at the same moment, turning our backs.

But what a difference three pints make. We just pulled our things off and scrambled awkwardly into pyjamas. We didn't stare at each other while we did this, but neither did we turn our backs. We both clocked the other's cock. Cocker's was a bit bigger than mine (with a name like that I supposed it would have to be) but not very much. I had nothing to feel intimidated about. We got into our separate beds, pulled the covers up, turned the lights out and said goodnight. Then Cocker said, 'Sweet dreams, and dry ones.'

'You too,' I said. I felt we were friends already. I snuggled down among the bedclothes with a warm safe feeling about Cocker that was really nice.

But an intake of three pints has other after-effects. Three times I had to get up and pee in the wash-basin, under the illumination of the shaving light. So did Cocker, which reassured me quite a lot. Otherwise I'd have felt a total dick. Actually, the third time I had to go, Cocker came and joined me at the sink. 'Sorry, mate,' he said. 'But needs must.' We pissed companionably for a minute, our two cocks hanging out of our pyjama gaps, just a few inches apart. At least, I thanked my stars, I didn't start to get stiff.

Back in bed again, the lights again off, Cocker spoke to me suddenly, taking me by surprise a bit. 'You know that Hamlet thing. Don't let those guys put you off. Just go for it. Not my thing, I don't think. But you... I think you should go along to the auditions and give it all you've got.'

'Thank you, Cocker,' I said. I could have hugged him for that. I hugged myself under the bed-clothes instead.

I don't think I'd have gone along to the auditions if Cocker hadn't said what he had said in the middle of the night. And he might not have said it at all if his bladder hadn't kept him awake. Funny how one thing hangs on another.

Even then I nearly didn't go. And even after I'd set out I nearly turned back at one point. A sharp east wind was blowing against me as I walked along Beaumont Street and I took it as a bit of a negative indication. I was trying hard to grow out of that tendency – the tendency to read signs and omens into everything that happened around me, especially negative things – but it was proving a bit of a battle. It was actually the thought of what Cocker would say if I had to tell him I'd chickened out that made me go on. No, not even that. I rather suspected that he'd be very sweet and understanding. That would have been even worse.

I pushed open the doors of the Playhouse and went inside. An arrow and the word Auditions had been drawn on a whiteboard propped up in the foyer. Approaching the room where I had to be, I was again overcome with panic. Coming through the wall was the sound of a man doing an audition piece at enormous volume and with great histrionic intensity. I thought, Oh shit, I can't do that... But I thought of Cocker again and went on in.

I did my usual party piece from A Midsummer Night's Dream. As Puck.

'Fairy, thou speak'st aright.
I am that merry wanderer of the night.
I jest to Oberon and make him smile
When I a fat and bean-fed horse beguile,
Neighing in likeness of a filly foal...'

I turned a cartwheel in the middle of the speech and they weren't expecting that. At least they'd remember my audition, I thought, even if I spent my three years here without ever getting a part.

'......... *and swear*

A merrier time was never wasted there.

But, room, fairy! here comes Oberon.'

'Thank you, Pip,' said a guy with a ponytail, who seemed to be in charge of things. He came up to me and handed me a book. 'That went well. Now could you read us a bit of this?'

I looked at the page. It was from Hamlet, Act I. 'Erm...' I hesitated. Most of the page was taken up with a longish speech by the Prince himself. 'Which bit do you want me to...?'

'From the Ghost's entrance,' said Ponytail casually. 'I'll cue you in. *Look, my lord, it comes.*'

And then I found myself doing it. As if I'd been pushed into deep water and was having to swim. '*Angels and ministers of grace defend us!*

Be thou a spirit of health or goblin damn'd,

Bring with thee airs from heaven or blasts from hell,

Be thy intents wicked or charitable...'

I expected to be stopped at any moment, but nobody stopped me. When I got to the end of the speech the ponytailed guy read the lines of Horatio's that came next, someone else did Marcellus, and I went on doing Hamlet's lines till the end of the scene.

Then we did stop. They said thank you again. They took my contact details. They'd be seeing other people, they said. They'd cast the play tomorrow. 'We'll let you know,' they said.

I left. I still didn't think I'd get a part. But at least I could look Cocker in the eye and tell him I'd done what he'd told me I should, and given it my best shot.

Cocker was busy polishing a pair of shoes when I got back. I hadn't seen anyone polish shoes since leaving school three months ago. I certainly hadn't polished any myself. He looked up as I came in. 'How did it go?' he asked.

I was touched that he remembered where I'd been. I was surprised at myself for being so touched. I said, 'They're letting us know tomorrow.'

'Then I'll keep my fingers crossed.' He went back to his shoes. 'Coming to the ball tonight?'

'Erm... no,' I said.

'Oh? Why not?' He looked up at me in surprise. There was also something else in that look that I couldn't quite identify. Though I knew I liked it, whatever it was.

'Oh, just this and that,' I said. 'Things to do.'

Of course I had nothing to do, beyond reading through a lot of paperwork to do with fees and battels and matriculation... And everyone including Cocker had to do that. He was kind enough not to pursue me down the cul-de-sac of my fib. He just said, 'Well, you can always change your mind. I think it'll be good. Good way to meet the chicks.'

'Yeah,' I said. 'Well, I might come along at the last minute.' Though I knew perfectly well I would not. I was terrified of the opposite sex. And my dancing was a mess.

I managed to disappear after dinner without running into Cocker again. He'd have tried to persuade me, from the kindest of motives, to come with him, and I'd either have given in and spent a miserable evening mortified by my own shyness, or puzzled him, maybe even hurt him a bit, by obstinately saying no.

Just about everyone was at the ball. Sitting alone in the room I shared with Cocker proved not to be much fun. I texted a few boys I'd been at school with, but none of them came back. They'd also all gone off to uni. They were probably each at their own freshers' dance.

I headed out into the dark streets. Most definitely everyone but me was dancing. There was nobody at all about.

I made my way past the Playhouse, where my future as a student actor would be decided in the morning. The thought of that made my breath come fast. I turned right, into Cornmarket Street, and then continued down St Aldates past Christchurch towards the river. There was a pub at the bottom, beside the bridge. The Head of the River, it was called. It was brightly lit and looked busy. I thought about going in, but I'd never gone into a pub on my own.

Instead I went out onto the bridge – Folly Bridge: I didn't know why it was called that – and stood there, listening to the water cascading over the weir below me, seeing its foam as dim white streaks in the dark.

I thought I'd dealt with the issue of homesickness when I'd gone away to boarding school all those years before. Thought I'd worked my way through it in my early years there. Thought it couldn't come back to haunt me, hurt me, ever again. At this moment I discovered that was not the case. The city around me was beautiful in the extreme, I gave it that. But it was alien to me. Whatever the opposite of home was, this was it.

I felt rather than saw that someone had come up and was standing beside me, leaning, as I was, over the parapet of the bridge. A male voice asked me, 'Are you all right?'

I looked up and turned towards the man. He looked to be in his early thirties. He smiled at me. He had a nice face, I thought. I said, 'Am I all right? I don't know.' And then it occurred to me to say something else. In a way I grew up in that moment. 'How about you?' I asked. 'Are you all right?'

Anthony McDonald

TWO

We sat in The Head of the River and talked. I had to suppose I'd been 'picked up'. I'd never been 'picked up' before. I'd assumed that when the time came for me to think about that idea it would be me doing the picking, and a girl – sorry, woman – who I picked up. Apparently not.

So far I couldn't fault the situation. Giles was a sensitive and charming man, and he'd bought me a drink. Remembering how incautious I'd been last night I asked for a half of lager and lime. He seemed quite pleased, I might even say reassured, by my choice. It probably chimed with his preconceptions about the kind of young man he would have hoped to meet, all alone and staring down into dark water from a bridge.

I thought him good-looking for his age. He was of medium height and stockily muscular. He had a Rugby player's physique. His eyes were warm brown twinkles shining out of a broad, almost Slavic-looking face. When he smiled he showed lovely teeth.

He worked in his father's business. They were funeral directors. He told me with a wry smile that it was a profession that was practically recession-proof. Your potential customers might choose a cheaper option, but the pool of prospects would never dry up. Then he gave a shrug. His job made him money, which everyone obviously wanted to have. But it wasn't very emotionally fulfilling, he said, and he was a creative type. 'I'm part of an amateur dramatic society,' he said. 'You might not think much to that, when you've got all your drama societies here at the university...'

I interrupted him. 'No, I think that's great. It's what I'd do if I was an undertaker … I mean a funeral director. I think it makes sense.' I told him I might or might not be a member of a university dramatic society. I'd know tomorrow, I said. There was a chance I'd land a small role in Hamlet.

He smiled at me very … tenderly might be the best word perhaps. 'I'm sure you'll land a part,' he said. 'That charm you have. That air of … gravity perhaps. Your smile is quite something. Has anyone ever told you that?' I shook my head. 'And there's a sort of vulnerability about you. You look … if I can put it like this … kind of cutely lost.' He looked at me a bit sideways, a bit shyly, as if to check how I was taking this. Then he took a swallow from his pint mug. I studied his profile. It was handsome, snub-nosed, full-lipped.

When he looked back at me he saw that my half-pint glass was nearly empty. He said, 'Can I get you another?'

I thought for a moment. Then I said, 'Yeah, that's kind of you. Would it be all right if I had a pint?' He seemed to have no problem with my request.

We were sitting side by side on a leather, button-back, bench seat. I noticed as we drank our second pint that, perhaps unconsciously, we'd swung round towards each other. We each had a knee up on the bench seat now. His right knee, my left. They were almost touching. But they did not touch. I realised then the full, aching meaning of *almost*. The cosmic gap that is *an inch apart*.

There was a wider gap than that between our legs, though. They yawned apart like steamed mussels, and stretched tight the fabric of our jeans across the crotch.

I told him, as I'd told Cocker last night, about my home on Exmoor. Out in the wilds rather – Lorna Doone country – he nodded – although, I admitted, I'd never managed to get through the book.

'People had longer attention spans then,' Giles said. 'Two hundred years ago. No telly. No internet.'

'My dad's a vet,' I told him. Cocker's dad was a doctor, he'd told me. I'd found that very reassuring. He'd know what to do if ever I was ill in the night.

'I live on my own at the moment,' Giles was saying. 'Would you like to come and see my place?'

I had to think about that for a moment. Giles gave me an amused smile – it was a very handsome pearly-white one – while I thought.

'Why not?' I said eventually. 'I think that would be nice.'

He had a house in Jericho. Jericho is the name of a little grid of streets just to the west of Walton Street. It was once terraces of workmen's cottages, but they became gentrified. My new friend Giles lived in one of the terraces. Jericho was pretty much round the corner from my own college, as it happened, which might turn out to be convenient – or not.

His place looked simple enough from the outside; it was beautifully furnished within. Antique tables and a dresser shared space with modern stuff. It was tasteful, yet comfortable at the same time. He ushered me into the main living-room. He didn't try to touch me while he was doing this. I respected him for that. Would I like a Jack Daniels? he asked me. I'd never had a Jack Daniels. I said yes.

We sat on the sofa, at opposite ends of it, but in the same position we'd got into in the pub. One knee each was up on the sofa, our crotches gaped. But the sofa was smaller than the pub seat, and this time our folded-on-the-sofa knees touched. It wasn't the first time my knee had accidentally, or half-accidentally, touched that of another boy or man. But it felt different this time. Probably because on neither of our parts was it an accident.

'Do you have a girlfriend back in Somerset?' Giles asked.

'No,' I said simply. 'I don't.' Then, remembering what I'd learned on my growing-up curve on the bridge a couple of hours earlier, I said, 'What about you?'

He shook his head and smiled. 'Nor me,' he said. 'Actually, I'm not into women all that much.'

'I don't think I am either,' I said, and was ashamed to hear my voice quaver as I spoke.

'We're all different, and it takes all sorts,' he said. I felt his knee give mine a tiny conspiratorial rub.

I said, 'You're gay, I suppose.'

'I'm into men rather than ladies,' he said, 'so I suppose, yes.'

'When did you know that?' I asked. 'When did you find out?'

'Is it important for you to know that?' His voice, like the Jack Daniels, was smooth and soft.

'Dunno,' I said. 'Maybe it is.' I started to tremble violently. I couldn't stop it. He could see that and, as his knee was pressed against mine, also feel it along his bones and sinews. He could feel it, as I could feel the pressure of his knee, all the way to the heart.

He said, 'I think you need holding for a minute. May I do that?' I nodded. He went on, 'I promise not to do anything that you don't want.'

I squirmed across the sofa towards him. With a bit of difficulty he wrapped his arms around me. I felt myself collapsing like a rag-doll onto his chest. I buried my face in his neck, which smelt wonderfully of a mixture of aftershave and himself, and burst into tears. I wanted Cocker suddenly. Before this moment I hadn't known that.

Giles rocked me to and fro very gently in his arms. Those arms of his seemed wonderfully big. One of them moved up my back and I felt his fingers stroke my hair. 'You're safe with me,' he said.

'Thank you,' I said. It came out on the end of a sob.

'I think you're a bit homesick,' Giles said.

'Perhaps you're right,' I said. That had been true on the bridge. It was more complicated now. Complicated by all sorts of things. Complicated by Giles. Complicated by Cocker. (I wanted a home with Cocker, I now realised.) Complicated by my dick, which was now rigid inside my pants. I said, 'Can you go on holding me for a bit?'

He squeezed me tight for a moment and I heard his breath intaken as a gasp. 'Oh, little angel,' he said, and I heard his voice start to break. He sounded very moved by what I'd said. 'I'll hold you as long as you want me to. Hold you all night if you want.' Then his chest started heaving and I realised he was crying silently inside himself. After a moment the heaving stopped. He said, 'And when you want me to, I'll let you go. Just say the word.' That last bit came out, I felt, through gritted teeth.

Actually I wanted to stay here all night. To stay exactly where I was, being held by him. Both of us keeping our clothes on. No homosexual activity would be taking place. I nudged my fully-clothed hard-on a little way into his crotch. 'Oh hey,' he said.

At some point in the night I was now envisaging, a night of having my hair stroked, of weeping intermittently against Giles's chest, of softly rubbing my crotch into his, I'd shoot my wad into my jeans, I realised, and Giles would notice that. I was only just eighteen, and that sort of thing still happened quite a lot. Giles was thirty-four, he'd told me. So that particular bit of awkwardness wouldn't happen to him while we lay here together tonight... But then, with another flash of intuition I realised that it well might.

Well, let it, I thought. If we both kept our clothes on it still wouldn't be a gay thing... I thought about Cocker, coming back to our room and finding me not there. He'd want to talk to me about the dance. He'd be let down if I wasn't there. No he wouldn't be. He might have pulled, have brought a girl back. Then he'd be glad I wasn't there. But in the morning he'd worry if I still wasn't back... I mean, he would, wouldn't he?

I wanted to talk to Cocker. He'd want to hear about what I'd got up to tonight. No, he wouldn't. And I couldn't possibly talk to him about it. I'd have to keep this bottled up inside me for the rest of my life. I wanted Cocker now. Wanted him desperately. I started crying again, letting the tears run down inside Giles's collar. He stroked my hair. He said, 'Just let it all out, little angel.' For answer I rubbed the bolt in my trousers up and down a few times against his midriff. He said, 'You can go on doing that all night too if you want.'

After half a minute I stopped the rubbing. After another half minute my tears trickled to a stop. I regained control over my breath and voice. We lay still together for about a minute after that. Then I sat up back from him. 'I think I ought to go,' I said.

'Whatever you like,' he said. I realised how difficult, and actually unselfish, it was of him to say that. Disappointment was in his face and in his voice.

I looked round at the little table beside my end of the sofa. I said, 'Would it be all right if I finished my Jack Daniels first?'

He gave a little laugh. 'Of course it's OK. You can have another one if you want.'

I said, 'I think I'll be OK just with this.'

We finished our drinks sitting demurely side by side, a whole foot of patterned sofa exposed between us. We spoke a bit. I don't know what we said. Then I got up. He got up too. Standing, I realised how visible my erection was, tenting my jeans as far as the material would stretch. Within those confines it was uncomfortably bent. With a shock I saw Giles's cock for the first time. It too was in his jeans, but he couldn't be wearing underpants It was standing to attention right behind his fly-zip. The top of it nearly reached the waistband. Mine never did that. His must be very big.

I walked past him towards the door and opened it. He didn't try to stop me or reach out to me, but he followed me to the door into the hall. When I'd gone through it I turned back to him. He was standing on his side of the doorway, his fingers hooked round the top of the lintel above his head as if he were going to do a set of pull-ups. He said, 'Will I see you?'

I said, 'I don't know.' I reached up with my hands and grasped the top of the lintel on my side of the door, mirroring his pose. 'I don't know,' I repeated. I got onto tip-toe as if launching myself into a pull-up, and thrust my hips forwards towards his. He did the same and I felt our hard cocks meet.

Our lips met a second later and we began to kiss. His lips were bigger, fleshier than mine. Very sensuous. They knew what they were about. Mine were still in the early stages of rehearsal. Then we came down from tiptoe, withdrew our hands from the lintel and wrapped them around each other, pulling our cocks and bellies towards each other. I felt our two ridges mash. I was conscious that his was twice as big. I ran my hands over the cheeks of his arse. How did I know to do that? Because there had been a boy at school who'd run his hands over mine. I knew how nice it felt.

Giles did the same to me. Then I felt the flat of his hand inside my waistband at the back and working its way like a tin-opener round to the front. If that was the next thing that one did... I followed suit.

A moment later I'd grasped his big cock. I felt a lurch of terrified pleasure in my gut. He was circumcised. I fingered the head of it, and was awed to find it wet. I got my hand around the shaft but my fingers and thumb barely met. It took Giles a moment longer to get his hand on my smaller, hooded number. He had to fumble his way into my underpants. It seemed he had dressed appropriately for the occasion; I had not.

In another second we would unzip each other. I knew that. There was a tense pause, like before the start of a race, and then we did. Our cocks and balls sprang out and their tips met.

I heard Giles's intake of breath. I heard my own. 'You're beautiful,' Giles said.

'So are you,' I said.

The next second I'd disengaged from him, was backing away and stowing away and zipping up. 'I'm sorry,' I said. 'I just meant to say goodbye.' I caught the catch of the front door and twisted it. It opened. 'Thank you,' I said.

As I went out I glanced back at him. His handsome cock was still standing, still out of his jeans, which were still unbuttoned at the top.

He didn't pursue me to the street door. 'Thank you, little angel,' he said. 'Come any time. You know where I live.'

My heart thumped loudly as I pulled the door to behind me and walked away along the street.

I threaded my way back to college. It wasn't far. I climbed the staircase and let myself into the room I shared. The light was on. Cocker was in bed, naked-shouldered, doing something with his i-Phone. Apart from that he was alone. He sat up a bit, turned and grinned at me. 'Hi there,' he said.

'How was the ball,' I asked.

'So-so,' he said. 'Danced with a couple of girls. Drank with a couple of blokes. You know what balls are like.'

I nodded and grunted an untruthful yes. I knew what my own balls were like, and now Giles's, but that was about it.

'Anyway, where did you get to?' he asked.

I shrugged in a manly sort of way. 'Oh, you know. I had some stuff to do. Phone friends. Paperwork. Later I went out for a walk. Got talking to a guy in a pub. Had a couple of pints... That's about it.'

Cocker looked up at me quizzically. 'Have you been crying?' he asked.

The defences I'd hastily erected gave way at Cocker's first gentle touch.

'Oh fuck, mate,' I said, and tears welled up all over again. Then, 'Cocker... Please can you give me a hug?'

I hadn't needed to ask, apparently. He was already out of bed, stark naked. He put his arms around me, outdoor jacketed as I was, and did just that. 'Tell me about it,' he said.

THREE

'Fuck it,' I said, 'It's difficult.'

His naked shoulders shrugged against my outdoor coat. 'What's new?' he said. He sat me down on his bed, then he sat next to me and wrapped an arm around my shoulder. He clasped his naked legs together for warmth, so tight that his cock and balls submerged between them so deep that he looked like a girl for a moment. He started to shiver then.

'You're cold,' I said. 'Put some clothes on.'

'Do you mind?' he asked. He unwrapped himself from me and hauled his pyjamas, blue and white striped, out from under his pillow. He started to put them on. Then I did – I said – the bravest thing I've ever done or said in my life. 'Or else we could just get into bed.'

He looked at me in astonishment. We were both standing beside his bed at this point. Me upright and fully clothed, he half in half out of pyjama bottoms, one knee raised, in arrested motion, like a figure from Pompeii. He didn't smile at me. He said, very seriously, 'Yes, we could. Do you want to take your clothes off first?'

I did, and I did.

I was lying naked under a duvet with a boy – a man, I mean – for the first time in my life. So was Cocker: I was quite certain about that. That I'd been upset about something, that he'd wanted me to tell him about the monumental things that had happened to me an hour earlier... Those things disappeared in smoke. The only thing, the wonderful thing that mattered now, was here I was, here Cocker was, smooth-skinned, nerve-endings on fire – both of us scared out of our wits – together in Cocker's bed.

He said, 'Are you cold?'

I said, 'No. Honestly.'

'It's just...'

'I know.' My teeth were chattering now.

'We're both shivering,' he said.

'I kn-n-now,' I said.

Neither of us knew what to do next. With Giles I'd somehow known the way things went. It had been like climbing a mountain up someone else's rope. I couldn't use that knowledge now; I don't know why that was. Cocker and I were climbing our own small mountain, but without guides, without way-points, without ropes. 'Can I put my arms around you?' I said. A moment ago, standing upright on our shared carpet, we'd been wrapped in a spontaneous embrace. Now it seemed I needed his permission. Now we were in his bed. But he didn't answer me. I took his silence as a yes.

I was right to do so, apparently. Because he wrapped his arms around me again. Neither of us said anything. Something deep inside me clanged like a great bell. It tolled a massive message. Treasure this moment. All through your life. Bigger things may happen. But this is the biggest yet.

Bold with beer and Jack Daniels I asked, 'May I touch your cock?'

He said, 'You probably shouldn't, but who am I to...?' He didn't finish the sentence in words. Instead I felt his hand, very bashfully, find its way around the base of my own penis before mine ever reached his.

My first wank with another boy. Cocker's too. It was a lovely thing, a beautiful thing, of course. We lay on our sides, tummy to tummy, one arm each wrapped affectionately around the other's neck and head. I felt the tension mount in Cocker's body. How easy it was to read his progress towards his climax, in the quaking of every part of him, in the sudden burgeoning of his shaft. He didn't speak or moan; neither did I. I felt the pulsing of Cocker's penis as he quickly brimmed and spilled. A second later I did the same. We flooded each other's tummy with our semen; it flowed down and wet Cocker's sheet.

There seemed too much to clear up, so we didn't even try to do that. We lay together in our cooling slipperiness. The phrase *cementing our friendship* swam into the receding tide of my wakefulness. I didn't attempt to voice it, thank God. We were closer, Cocker and I, than either of us had ever been to another person as, in each other's arms, we drifted towards sleep.

We woke in the small hours. Our arms had gone numb and we both needed to piss. As we stood together at the wash-basin Cocker said, 'We shouldn't have done that.' In a rueful tone of voice and minutely shaking his head.

'I know,' I said. 'It wasn't right.' But I was lying. Lying to Cocker, lying to myself. I knew I was. So had Cocker also been lying? To me and to himself? And if so, did he also know that he was? I couldn't possibly ask. So what he'd said hurt me dreadfully. I felt that with his words he'd cast me – and I with my reply had cast him – into a hideous pit. 'I'd better get back to my own bed,' I said. There was no enthusiasm in my tone as I said that, but Cocker didn't try to talk me out of it. He just grunted, and I walked over to my cold un-slept-in sheets and duvet, while he went back to his. At least his was still a warm, if sex-stained place to sleep in. I couldn't help feeling that in that, at least, he had the best of it.

In the morning, we were still speaking, at least. We were still friendly and polite. But there was something brittle and artificial in the way we talked together. We wanted to make the best of it. I knew I did, and it was clear from his behaviour that Cocker also did. We walked together to breakfast in hall and pointedly sat next to each other. Back in our room we took it in turns to go to the loo, and we brushed our teeth. Somehow we didn't seem to want to be far apart. It was an odd way to behave, come to think of it, given that we both thought we'd wrecked our friendship by doing what we'd done last night. Sometimes our body language can be more truthful than our deepest feelings, a better pointer to reality than our sincerest thoughts.

An email popped up on my phone just then. It was from the dramatic society. I'd expected just a short text.

I nearly dropped the phone as I read it. The part of Hamlet was between me and one other person. Would I come and read again, please? If I didn't get the part of Hamlet I'd be absolutely sure of getting something else pretty major. Meanwhile, they hadn't found a Horatio yet. Did I know anyone by any chance...?

I was too excited to try to say any of this to Cocker. I made him read the email for himself. 'Christ, you've done well for yourself,' he said. Forgetting himself for a moment he ruffled my hair and said, 'I'm fucking proud of you, mate.'

I willed away the tears that threatened to spring. I said, 'You ever do any acting at school?'

He sort of wriggled his head. 'A bit,' I suppose.

'Come with me,' I said. 'Read for Horatio.'

'Bloody hell, mate,' he said. 'I'm not in that league... Anyway, it's not one of the things I came here for. No plans to be a thesbian,' he said.

'Thespian,' I said. It struck me very forcefully that Cocker would make a perfect Horatio. It struck me less than a lightning flash later that if I was Hamlet and Cocker was Horatio that would be the most wonderful thing that could happen in all the world. Of course I had no idea at all if Cocker could act... 'Just come with me anyway,' I said. 'At the very least you'll be there for moral support. And you'll bring me luck.'

I saw that look in his blue eyes again. The look I couldn't explain or interpret. I only knew I liked it. Actually *liked* seemed by now a bit of an understatement.

We walked together to the Playhouse. Mr Ponytail met us in the foyer. He seemed delighted to see me and also pleased that I'd brought a friend. He took us with him into the auditorium. Unlike yesterday's, this morning's auditions were being held on the stage. The space, and the acoustic, were alarmingly big. We looked around us, awestruck. Then Cocker did a lovely thing. He looked me in the eye and smiled and said, 'Don't worry. You'll be all right, mate.'

The next bit wasn't so good. We had to sit and listen while, up on the stage ahead of us the other candidate for Hamlet strutted and fretted his way through To be or not to be. He was a big and handsome chap, with a big voice. He was also rather good. It was intimidating for both of us. I could see Cocker feeling intimidated: it was written in the way he tightly crossed his legs.

Then Ponytail handed a copy of the script to me and another to Cocker. He pointed with a finger to the place. We stood up and walked up the aisle, then up steps onto the stage. The other Hamlet was coming down. 'Good luck, guys,' he said.

'And well done, you, mate,' we both said to him. Now we were up on stage, Cocker and I, beneath the gaping fly tower overhead, at the centre of the big bare space. Our nerves and apprehensions vanished suddenly. We stood there together comfortably, companionably, the way we'd stand chatting at the wash-basin, or beside Cocker's bed. I began, 'We'll teach you to drink deep ere you depart.' I gave Cocker a little nod.

'My lord, I came to see your father's funeral,' Cocker said. He was reading from the page of course, but it didn't sound like it, and it didn't look like it. Our eyes met.

'I pray thee, do not mock me, fellow-student; I think it was to see my mother's wedding,' I said.

'Indeed my lord,' said Cocker, 'it followed hard upon.'

Spontaneously I let out a bitter laugh. 'Thrift, thrift, Horatio,' I said. 'The funeral baked meats did coldly furnish forth the marriage table...' I gave a sudden start. 'My father, methinks I see my father.'

Cocker laid a reassuring hand on my forearm for a second. 'Oh. Where, my lord?

'In my mind's eye, Horatio,' I said.

'I saw him once,' said Cocker. 'He was a goodly king.'

I said, 'He was a man, take him for all in all. I shall not look upon his like again.'

Cocker seemed to puff himself up. 'My lord, I think I saw him yesternight...'

We went on. The dialogue opened out into Horatio's first big speech. I wondered how Cocker would handle that. It was like watching a river boat head out into the wide open sea...

Cocker didn't act. He didn't need to. He just was Cocker. And Cocker was Horatio. Horatio and Hamlet, in natural unforced conversation together, were, it turned out, no more nor less than Cocker and me.

Ponytail stopped us after a while. 'What can I say?' he said. 'The chemistry between you two...'

The other Hamlet stepped up beside him. 'You win hands-down,' he said to me. He nodded towards Cocker. 'Though without your friend here I might have given you a better run for your money.' He came between us and drew us close towards him, a big arm around each of our shoulders. 'I look forward to working with you both. I'm playing Claudius. It's the role I really wanted actually. I'm Will.' Then he turned on his heels and left.

We'd got the parts. It felt like we hadn't even tried for them. That they'd just fallen into our laps. Rehearsals would start in a few days, Ponytail told us, at the end of Freshers' Week.

In a daze we walked out of the Playhouse and into Beaumont Street. We had that disoriented feeling you get when you come out of a daytime screening of a movie and are surprised to see the daylight, and ordinary things happening, in the street. Ponytail – actual name James – had used the expression, What can I say? It also applied to us. We had no words to say to each other as we stood on the pavement, unsure whether we were going to walk somewhere together – and if so, where that somewhere would be – or if we were going to split.

We checked our phones. It was a way of putting decisions off. I found I'd got an answer to one of the messages I'd sent last night. I'd deal with it later. Cocker seemed to be going through the same routine. He put his phone away. He said, 'I know it's early,' (it was just gone midday) 'but d'you think we ought to celebrate with a drink?'

As it happened, I did think that.

We turned right, and headed into St Giles. In a moment we were outside the Lamb and Flag. It was the only pub we'd been to together. The last time we'd been two among six. Now there was something special and unusual about the feeling I got as we went through the door together. Just the two of us.

'I'll get these,' Cocker said as we walked to the bar with a bit of a swagger. He got his wallet out.

We sat down with a pint in front of each of us at a small table near the bar. We touched our glasses and said cheers. I risked it. 'Been a bit of an eventful twelve hours,' I said.

I could see from his face that I'd stepped a bit too far across a line whose position had not yet been accurately fixed. 'Hmm,' he said. It was as if he'd been a snail and I'd flicked a bit of salt at him.

'Sorry,' I said, backing off. 'I didn't mean to say that.'

He ignored that. He gave me a rather searching look. He said, 'Last night you were a bit upset about something. You never got round to telling me what it was.'

I laughed uncomfortably. 'Oh nothing,' I said. 'I'd almost forgotten it.' I found myself transported back to Folly Bridge, looking down at the white streaks of foam glimmering in the dark. 'Water under the bridge.'

FOUR

Other things than auditions and pub visits took place during Freshers' Week. There were library tours, welcome meetings from a whole host of societies, and a lot of academic stuff, plus getting to know the tutors and fellow-students who were involved in the subjects we were going to read. Cocker was here to read Economics, I was reading Modern History. We had different agendas over the next few days. We didn't spend much of our daytimes together for the rest of Freshers' Week. We went to different places. We made different new friends.

We didn't let go of our old friends, though. I quickly replied to the text I'd got from one of them. His name was Alex, and he'd gone to Southampton to read medicine. At school we'd been very close. He it was who had groped my bum on one occasion when, a little overcome with high summer, lager and lime and emotion, we'd given each other a goodnight hug outside a pub.

Actually we'd done slightly more than that. For years I'd admired his looks and physique. I suspected now that the converse had also been the case. But on that evening of heightened feeling, out on the pavement, embracing a bit tentatively, we hadn't quite stopped at a one-way bum caress. I'd groped him back, in the same place. Then he'd given me an experimental peck on the cheek. In return I'd pecked his. I'd liked the feel of that. The nerve endings in my lips and cheek still remembered it. We'd then both switched our attention to the other's trouser front. Simultaneously a hand of his, a hand of mine, had found the top of the other's thigh and started to stroke that. We were a second away from feeling for the other's cock. We'd have found them both hard if we had done. It was I who'd stopped it. 'Better not,' I said, and reluctantly we dis-embraced.

His text gave an account of the Freshers' Ball at Southampton that was even terser than Cocker's account of the one at Oxford. *Danced w a girl – Alice – v nice.* Alex and Alice, I thought. There were pros and cons to that combination of names, if it took off. That made me think of another combination of names. Pip and Cocker. Cocker and Pip... I texted back to Alex. *Roomie called Cocker. In a play together. Hamlet. Me Hamlet – believe or not.*

Alex texted back. *He Ophelia? Await news on this.*

I thought of the tumultuous events of the last couple of days. There was no way I'd be telling Alex about that. Certainly not by text. Perhaps when – if – we met face to face at Christmas. Even then it was still perhaps. Until then I was on my own with all of it. Whatever the *all of it* was.

I came in early one evening to find Cocker entertaining a girl in our shared bedroom. She had long blonde hair, wore a sky blue jumper and very tight jeans with pink stitching all down and across the legs. They were having coffee. I was introduced and made a little small-talk. After a few minutes I made an excuse and left. I went and called on a fellow member of my History group. He was a rather unexciting sort of chap called Michael. I guessed he wouldn't be doing anything more interesting than sitting in his own room, and he was not. We chatted quite pleasantly about books and coursework until the chimes of Old Tom, floating over the rooftops of the old town, told us that dinner time was approaching.

Cocker was sitting next to the girl at dinner. I joined a different table, and sat with other people I was getting to know and, maybe, like. By bedtime the girl had vanished. Cocker did mention her in passing as we chatted about this and that before getting into our separate beds. He didn't exactly dwell on her though, and I too was quite happy to let the matter drop.

Next day I joined one of the tours of the Bodleian Library. An extraordinary building, it dated from the reign of James the First and Sixth. Its nearly windowless façades were – are – decorated in what looks like linen-fold panelling carved in solid stone. It must have taken an age to do. But time was experienced differently in those days, I thought. We never seemed to have enough of it, they seemed almost to have had too much.

'Hi,' a girl's voice – woman's voice, sorry – said to me quietly. 'We're in the same college, I think.'

I turned and recognised her. She'd been on the table at which I'd sat last night. I'd thought her pretty then. She looked even prettier close up. 'Yes, I've seen you,' I said. I gave her one of my special smiles which I like to think charm everyone, though sometimes I've been wrong about that.

We got into a conversation, although rather quietly. We were supposed to be listening to a librarian explaining the system for using and borrowing books.

She was mightily impressed when I told her I'd landed the part of Hamlet on my third day at Oxford. We sat together that night at dinner. After dinner I invited her out for a drink.

I didn't want to take her to the Lamb and Flag in case Cocker was there. He or others among my new mates. I took my courage in both hands, and, praying that my wallet would stand it, took her to into the Morse bar at The Randolph instead.

Nice girls are the ones who, when offered a drink in a shockingly posh bar by someone very young and penniless, choose a half of lager in preference to the double Malibu and Coke they know they really want. My new friend was a nice girl. Her name was Cate.

We had a lot of things in common. She too lived in deep countryside. She too had a parent – though it was her mother in her case – who was a vet. We sat talking long enough for me to have downed about three pints had I been with Cocker – or Giles – but I stayed spinning out my own half of lager, drinking at Cate's pace. They say that women are are a restraining, civilising influence on the male sex. I began to see the truth of that.

I told her I shared a room in college but for some reason couldn't bring myself to tell her what my room-mate's name was. She let slip – she got it into the conversation seamlessly – that she had a room all to herself. So when our drinks were finished it seemed perfectly natural that it was she who asked me if I'd like to come back to her place for coffee rather than the other way around.

As we walked towards the door of the Morse bar I spotted Giles sitting at a table, opposite a young man. It gave me a bit of a jolt. The young man was younger than Giles but older than me. Giles saw me. He gave me a half-wave that the young man he was with didn't even clock. I gave Giles a half-wave that Cate didn't clock.

Her room was on a staircase in the oldest part of the college. Most of the main building dated from the eighteenth century, but there was one wing that still survived from the middle ages. It only survived because the eighteenth century re-builders ran out of money to pull it down and replace it, as they had done with the rest of the place. They must have been embarrassed by this relic of the dark ages, surviving to mock the lop-sided grandeur of the new part. But now, in the twenty-first century, it was the most sought-after part of the college when it came to choosing a room. Funny how things work out.

It was very quaint and charming, the room she took me into. It had stone-mullioned windows and small panes of glass. It also had a very small sofa in it, instead of the two armchairs that Cocker and I had in ours. I sat on the sofa, at one end of it, while Cate made coffee for us both. When she came back with a mug for each of us she had the choice of sitting on the hard chair at her desk, or next to me on the sofa, or else on the bed.

She came and sat next to me on the sofa. It was little more than half the size of Giles's sofa, so that we found ourselves sitting very close. She looked at me and smiled silently, almost expectantly. I knew the next move was mine. I just didn't know what the move was. I wondered what Cocker would have done. I needed him to tell me what to do.

Perhaps the thing to do was to put my hand on her leg and up under her skirt. But perhaps you weren't supposed to do that. At least, not at first. The top of her dress was fastened with a series of either clips or poppers at the back. Maybe the thing was to get those undone somehow and then tackle one of her bra-straps. Women liked to have their breasts fondled, and men liked to fondle them. I thought I would like that.

But maybe you were supposed to start with a kiss. I decided this was the safest route. I leaned in towards her. She smiled at me. Encouraged, I planted a smacking kiss on her lips.

She tried to turn her head aside but was too late. My lips met hers fair and square. The flat of her hand made contact with my cheek.

It doesn't hurt much when a woman slaps your face. But that's small consolation. The humiliation of the thing is something else.

'I'm sorry,' I said. 'I got that wrong, obviously.'

She almost laughed. 'I think you did.'

I got up. 'I guess I'd better be going,' I said.

'It's OK,' she said. 'It's just that that was a bit soon, when we've only just met.'

'I understand,' I said. I wanted to die.

'Stay and finish your coffee anyway,' Cate said.

Good God, I thought. Weren't women supposed to be the intuitive ones? The ones who somehow understood? I realised now that they understood nothing about men. They understood me even less than I did. And that was saying something. I didn't understand myself one bit. 'I'll go, I think,' I said. I made a final effort to right my capsized dignity. 'See you some other time, I hope.'

'I hope so too,' she said.

I was floored by that. I had no answer to it. I was by the door and turning the handle. 'Goodnight,' I said, and walked out. The staircase seemed even narrower, darker and more twisted than when I'd come it. It was the staircase of my defeat.

Outside in the open air I felt slightly better. But I wasn't ready to go back to my room yet. I couldn't face the place on my own, if Cocker wasn't there. But if he was in already … well, I couldn't face him either just yet. That he might be up there but not alone, that he might have female company with him, that was a possibility too uncomfortable to contemplate. I decided not to contemplate it. I made my way out of the college grounds and went for a walk round the lamp-lit streets instead.

I walked down Walton Street and into Jericho. I was curious – only curious, mind: no more than that – to see if I could remember in which house Giles lived. I found it almost more easily than I'd thought possible. It seemed almost to leap out at me around the corner of one of the little streets. I re-memorised its number, just in case. I looked at the windows. There was a light in the hall, I noticed, and light came also from between thick curtains at the window of the sitting-room where, two nights earlier, I had sat with Giles … and we had done a little more than that.

I stood close to that window and listened carefully. I could hear no sound. No people talking. No TV. No music playing. No way of telling if Giles was at home alone, or if he was sharing his end of evening with the young friend I'd seen him with at the Randolph. Or whether he'd simply left the light on as a precaution, to pretend for the benefit of snoopers that the house wasn't empty. Perhaps he was still out at the Randolph. Or elsewhere in the town. Short of knocking on the door I had no way of knowing – and I certainly wasn't going to do that.

I pressed on through Jericho until the quarter disgorged me on the canal bank. By now I thought I was just about ready to turn for home – I meant my college – and face what awaited me there, whether that meant Cocker, or Cocker's absence, or even Cocker with a woman in his bed.

I wasn't alone on the tow-path. Young people of both sexes, students I supposed, were using it as a short cut home to the various places where they lived. At one point I passed two young guys walking with an arm around each other. For a second I thought they might be Giles and his young man. They were not. They were younger than that. But the encounter gave me a feeling I hadn't expected. It was like nothing I'd experienced before. It gave me a kind of frisson, a kind of pang, as if I'd tasted something sharp on my tongue.

The tow-path took me round the outside of the wall that enclosed my college grounds, then brought me past a line of painted narrow-boats out into Hythebridge Street. From there it was just a few minutes till I was back. I went in and climbed my stairs. I'd beaten Cocker to it. He wasn't in yet. I wasn't sure if I was glad of that or not.

It was bedtime by now. I pottered about the room for a minute before taking my clothes off and while I was pottering the door opened and Cocker walked in. I realised I was very glad of that. A look on his face told me he was equally pleased to see me. He drew breath to ask me what I'd been doing. I know that because I drew breath to ask him what he'd been doing. But then we both thought better of it. I know we both did. I read it in his face. He read it in mine. We'd quickly grown transparent to each other. Though only up to a point...

We talked of other things. Just silly things, like the tea supply, the toilet-paper situation, and what we had to do tomorrow. Then we got undressed. Last night we'd been coy about this because we'd been to bed together and had sex the night before that. Tonight by contrast we weren't shy about this. Probably because we hadn't been to bed together yesterday. We'd laid a fire-break, if you like, between us and that moment: a moment that we now thought (or thought we thought) had been a bit too intimate. So as we took our kit off we openly glanced at each other's naked form and half-jutting cock. Not for so long as to count as staring, or dwelling on what we saw. Just long enough to take in – and secretly approve – the sight. We made no comment on each other's appearance though, but performed our night-time ablutions quietly and got into our respective beds. We said goodnight and turned the lights off.

About five minutes later I found there was something I needed to do. I wasn't sure, though, how to go about it. It was the age-old problem that every boarding-school boy knew about. (Plus, I guessed, a lot of other boys who, unlike me, hadn't gone to boarding school.) Did you do it brazenly, untroubled by the knowledge that your room-mate would hear you doing it, or as quietly as possible, so as not to give yourself away?

I mulled over this question for a minute or two, during which time my cock grew ever more stiff. But then the answer presented itself. I heard very soft but unmistakeable sounds coming from Cocker's bed. Cocker was quietly, but not entirely silently, starting to masturbate.

If he could do it I could do it. I pulled my pyjama trousers down below my knees. (Don't know why we all like to do that. But we just do, somehow, even if the evolutionary point of it doesn't spring to mind immediately.) Then I went for it, lying under the duvet on my back. I didn't do it noisily or attention-seekingly. But neither did I try to do it in silence. I did it more or less the way Cocker was doing it in fact. Under both duvets there was a certain amount of twitching of legs.

Eventually I shot off up my tummy under my pyjama top. I knew I was thinking about Cocker, imagining him doing the same thing at the same moment as I did. A minute later I pulled my bottoms back up but apart from that left everything as it was. By this time Cocker had also finished and quietened down. I didn't hear him groping for tissues or a handkerchief. I wondered if he had dealt with his spunk exactly as I had done with mine. The thought made me smile involuntarily. My fondness for him went to a new level at that moment. A warm glow spread through my being. I felt an inner me hugging an inner him. To my surprise I felt his name forming soundlessly on my lips.

FIVE

Oh God, Oh God! How weary, stale, flat and unprofitable seem to me all the uses of this world...

'Tis an unweeded garden that grows to seed; things rank and gross in nature possess it merely... Within a month – frailty, thy name is woman – a little month, or ere those shoes were old, with which she followed my poor father's body, like Niobe, all tears, why she – even she ... married with mine uncle.

Rehearsals had started. Other things had started too. The Michaelmas term. Lectures. Tutorials. Seminars. They should have been important, all those things. They were not. It was the production of Hamlet that seized every moment of my consciousness. Why should this be? It was just a student production, after all. I was merely a student Prince. It was Cocker, of course, who clinched it...

Do I need to explain that? I'll try. In only a few scenes of Hamlet do the prince and his best mate appear together. Yet whenever we did those scenes or parts of scenes in rehearsal the atmosphere went high voltage. Cocker and I were not in love. We both knew that. Yet when we appeared on stage together the impression we gave was that my Hamlet and Cocker's Horatio were very much in love together, yet repressing it. Our director, James (I'll stop calling him Mr Ponytail) certainly thought so, and so did the other members of the cast.

'How are you trying to say it?' Cocker asked me after I'd done that speech for the first time. 'Tis an unweeded garden that grows to seed, I mean. Do you mean – unweeded gardens in general grow to seed? Or that the world is an unweeded garden?'

James never went into such nit-picky detail as that.

'I was trying to get both ideas across,' I flannelled.

'That's what it sounded like,' said Cocker. 'Result: you got neither of them across. You kind of fell between the two.'

'I'll think about it,' I said, 'and make up my mind, and come back with something stronger next time.'

I loved it when Cocker criticised my acting. How many reasons there were for that! It was wonderful, for a start, that he knew how to, and did it well. It was wonderful that he dared to, when nobody else – not even James – did. I loved it that he cared enough. That he watched me that closely...

In return I criticised the way he delivered a line sometimes. He seemed to love that minor bruise upon his ego as much as I loved it when he criticised me. I've mentioned that warm feeling I got inside myself when things were said between us. I've also mentioned the transparency through which we seemed to look into each other's thoughts and heart. Put those two things together... I knew that the warm feeling was his too...

Reader, you're ahead of me and Cocker at this point. You know what all that was about. What those symptoms pointed to. Up to this moment we did not.

I was sky-high at the end of that first rehearsal day. Even better, I knew that Cocker was. We sat together in hall at dinner. I said, 'Fancy going out for a few beers? Bit of a day to celebrate?'

He pulled a face. 'Actually, I said I'd have a drink with Eleanor...'

Eleanor? I thought. Who the fuck is that? Then I remembered. She was the girl – I mean woman – who was playing Ophelia. I'd thought her very attractive when we'd met. But this moment changed all that. A tiresome, tedious, rather plain-faced person, I now thought.

'Fine,' I said. 'Good for you, mate. Get lucky. We'll have that drink another night.' We certainly would, I thought.

I went out for a walk on my own, through the dark streets. I stood on Folly Bridge for ages, looking at the white-streaked darkness tumbling noisily below. I wondered if anyone would come up and talk to me. Cocker perhaps. Or Giles. Or Alex, all the way from Southampton!! Or anybody at all, in fact. But nobody did. I plucked up the courage to walk into The Head of the River. I glanced around me as I trawled the bars. Nobody was there. I mean, nobody who mattered. Nobody I recognised.

Back up Cornmarket Street. (I was learning to call it The Corn.) Left into Beaumont Street. I looked in at The Randolph. No Giles tonight. No Cocker with … what was her name? Continuing down Beaumont Street... The college stood ahead of me, the clock in the Georgian pediment above its front gate reminding me the night was yet young. I didn't go in. At the last moment I veered away to the right, along Walton Street, towards Jericho.

No sound came from inside the house. Light bled out around the edges of the curtains in the window of the living-room. I hadn't looked before, hadn't registered whether there was a knocker or a bell. Now I did. It was a knocker. A brass one, with a laurel-wreathed head on it. Wake Duncan with thy knocking, I thought. I hammered hard enough to cry the whole street to wake.

The door opened. Giles stood there. He was in jeans, and a white woollen something like a sort of cardigan, but open so that his bare chest showed underneath. He looked very good, I thought. He didn't look angry at having his peace disturbed. Nor terribly surprised. But nor was he transfigured by joyous ecstasy, I have to admit. Pleased. And amused. Those adjectives come nearest to describing his state. 'You've found me again, little angel,' he said. 'You'd better come in, I think.'

Sometimes I still felt like a kid. Sometimes that was a good feeling. Sometimes it was not. Sometimes it was a bit of both. Now was one of those bit-of-both times. I almost skipped through the hall and into the sitting-room. I'd only been here once but I behaved as if I knew the house well. As if I belonged here with Giles. I sort of jumped onto the sofa. At the same end I'd sat upon before.

Giles didn't join me on the sofa. He stayed standing. He was trying to look a bit serious – a bit concerned for my youthful welfare – but the corners of his mouth kept turning up. He said, 'You look as though you could do with a drink.'

'Do you have any of that Jack Daniels stuff?' I asked him.

Turned out he did.

It was funny how our bodies seemed to have remembered things, and to have remembered them the same. Once our drinks were poured we found ourselves sitting knee to knee on the sofa again: that is, with one knee tucked up and touching, the other flung wide, foot on the floor beside.

'So tell me, what's been happening to you?' Giles asked.

'I suppose there's quite a bit,' I said.

'It's only been three days,' Giles said.

'I kissed a girl for the first time in my life and got my face smacked,' I said.

'Happens to everyone,' Giles said, poker-faced.

'My room-mate and I have both got parts in Hamlet,' I told him.

'Playing what?' Giles asked.

I found it difficult to hit the right tone of voice for this next bit. 'I'm playing Hamlet,' I said.

He reached out a hand and took mine and gently squeezed it. He said quietly, 'Congratulations, kid.' Then he grinned naughtily. 'Your room-mate's giving his Ophelia, perhaps?'

I refused to take the joke. 'Oh Christ,' I said. 'Why does everyone say that?'

'I'm sorry, Pip,' Giles said contritely. 'I didn't know everyone was saying that. Perhaps I should have thought. I apologise for being a plouc.'

'What's a plouc?' I asked him.

'Doesn't matter,' he said. 'It's French.'

I sat up, leaned a little way towards him along the sofa. 'I didn't mean to be spiky,' I said. I rested the palm of my left hand on his right thigh. 'It's just that he's gone out drinking with the girl who *is* playing Ophelia tonight.'

Giles gave me a rather roguish look. 'Shit happens,' he said. There was silence for a bit as we slurped our Jack Daniels, thought the silence wasn't complete. The ice in our glasses bangled around a bit.

'This room-mate of yours,' Giles said. 'What's he like?'

'We've slept together,' I said.

'I see,' said Giles soberly. There was a pause. Then, 'He sounds nice.'

'He is,' I said.

'What's his name?' Giles asked.

'Cocker,' I said.

Giles didn't laugh. I respected him for that. He leaned forward and ran his hand up over my jeans, up the inside of my thigh, till the flat of his hand saucered my cock. Then his fingers found my zip toggle and tweaked it down slowly, cautiously. I found I had no objection to that.

In my turn I reached for Giles's fly and inched that down. 'Sauce for the goose...' I said. I realised for the first time that no line was too cheesy when you were about to have sex.

Nothing happened at that point. Both of us were wearing underpants, so nothing popped out and up. There was a moment's hiatus as we took on board the fact that my underwear was sky blue and his was black. Then Giles said, 'Are you OK if I ask you to come upstairs?' I looked around anxiously at my drink. 'Bring that.' he said. I did.

In the bedroom we kissed briefly. Then we undressed ourselves, not each other, but we watched each other very attentively while we did that. As Giles's physique revealed itself I liked it more and more. He looked more like an Olympic swimmer than an undertaker, and I was glad of that. His cock – well, that was massive, and … OK, I was very turned on by that.

Giles was the first to sit on the bed. He caught my hand and pulled me down till I sat beside him. Then he leant down into my lap and took my cock in his mouth. Nobody had done that before, and I'd never been double-jointed enough to do it to myself. The sensation was more than unexpected. It was electric. My whole body convulsed. 'Fuck, wow,' I said.

He released me from his mouth gently, like a gun-dog dropping a bird it has picked up. Then he rolled me backwards onto the bed, and rolled himself over to the other side of me so that for a moment we were lying side by side on our backs. 'Lie on my tummy,' he said quietly. I obeyed him, rolling back sideways until I was on top. Belly to belly, chest to chest, cock to cock and lips to cheek.

How warm Giles's body felt. How comforting, how strong, yet soft. I hadn't got into quite this position with Cocker. Next time I would... A pang went through me. We'd more or less agreed there wouldn't be a next time. He'd gone out with a girl tonight... I returned my attention to the present. This moment with Giles. This should surely be good enough. I felt the ridge of my erection pressing hotly into my tummy. I felt the longer thicker one that Giles had, right alongside mine, doing the same thing. I felt them both pulse.

Giles said, 'Oh hey, you're dripping!'

I was mortified. 'Sorry Giles,' I said.

I felt Giles's arms tighten around me as he laughed. 'Don't be sorry, don't be silly, little angel; it's lovely, I like it, it's nice. Another second and I'll be doing the same, don't worry.' Another second and I wormed my hand in between us to find out if he was right. I found that he was.

I didn't know what to do at that point. I just lay on top of Giles, enjoying the closeness and the safety, the warm softness and the hot hardness, and waited for him either to tell me what to do next or else make a move himself. He neither moved nor spoke. Eventually I said, 'What should I do now?'

Giles said quietly, 'When we were on the sofa a few days ago you pushed your crotch into mine and humped me for a bit. Although we had our clothes on I think we both liked that. It's even better naked. Why don't you go for that?'

Without raising my body from his I started to thrust, or rather twitch, my hips. It worked wonderfully. I hadn't realised how wet we had both got. My prick slid easily up and down against his belly while at the same time my belly massaged his prick.

'That feels lovely,' I said.

'Of course it does,' Giles said. 'And not just for you, in case you were wondering.'

'I was wondering,' I said. Though I might not have been speaking the truth.

'You could come inside me if you like,' Giles said.

'Inside you?' I queried. I kept on thrusting, sliding up and down his belly, as I spoke.

'Just slide back down a bit, then push up again between my legs. You'll slide in easily, I promise.' What he meant by that last bit, I realised, was that I wasn't very big.

He'd made me feel very nervous. 'I don't think I'm ready for that yet,' I said. I think what I meant was that I didn't think I was gay enough.

'That's fine,' he said. 'Just keep on going the way you are. Come on my tummy. I want that.'

I felt my excitement suffuse me as it bubbled up. I said, almost without breath, 'I think I'm nearly ready to go now.'

He said, 'Then go for it. Let me feel your hot spunk.'

His words might have been cheap and cheerful but they certainly had an impact on my cock. I felt my semen rising deep inside me. Involuntarily I doubled the speed of my now squirming thrusts. I heard Giles's breath knocked out of him by the pounding of my chest against his.

I didn't say anything more to announce my coming. He could hardly fail to notice when I shot. When I'd finished I sort of flopped on top of him. 'Well done, angel,' he said, and stroked my hair. Then he wriggled his other hand in between us to keep himself going now that I'd stopped moving about.

It didn't seem very comfortable or effective, so after a moment or two I knelt up, my knees planted on the bedclothes, between his thighs to give his wrist and cock a bit more space. I saw approvingly that I'd made the whole of his belly and chest glisten with my wash. I stroked the sensitive insides of his thighs and then his balls, which he was wearing high and tight.

I thought it might take him a long time to reach his climax, since he was a good deal older than I was, and

I'd read that was often the case. But actually it was probably less than a minute before he gasped and spasmed, and I saw his sperm arc out.

He grinned up at me, then said, 'There's a box of tissues down there.' He pointed down beside the bed. I reached and got them, handed the box to him, and he did most of the rest. 'Now shall we finish our drinks?' he said.

I was almost ready to run off into the night again at that point, and I could see that he knew that was the case. Perhaps for that reason I refrained from panicking. 'Yeah, let's do that, I said.'

He got out from between my legs and went and got a couple of dressing-gowns. He wrapped himself in one of them and draped the other around me, in the process taking the opportunity to tweak my waning but still wet dick.

We went downstairs again, taking our drinks. We returned to the sofa. This time I leant backwards into Giles's lap, and he cradled me with his arms, brushing the nape of my neck with his lips. 'What happened when you went to bed with Cocker?' he asked me.

'We wanked each other under his duvet,' I said. It was wonderful to have told someone that. 'We went to sleep in each other's arms, still wet.'

'Sounds lovely,' said Giles. 'But why, now you've done it once, aren't you doing it every night?'

'He's into girls,' I said.

'He's probably into trying a bit of everything,' Giles said. 'Give him a bit of time, I suggest. He may need a bit of a breathing space after what happened between you. But I wouldn't give up hope on that front yet.'

I began to get drowsy in Giles's arms. I thought I wanted to spend the night like this, cuddling on his sofa in dressing-gowns, or naked in his bed. But then thoughts of Cocker obtruded. I didn't like the idea of leaving him lonely in our bedroom, wondering what had happened to me. Of him, waking in the morning to find me still not back.

Of course I might go back and find his bed empty, or with him and Eleanor together in it. I might wake and find him still absent. But those were risks I'd have to take. There's no wanting without a risk attached. No getting without hurting. Love – if that's what I was beginning to feel for Cocker – comes with an eye-watering price-tag attached.

I said, 'I need to go now. Thank you. It's been nice.'

Giles said. 'You need to get home to Cocker. I know that.' He gave me a final squeeze and then we both got up. 'Get dressed upstairs,' he said. 'Without me watching you. Otherwise the temptation to keep you here all night will be impossible to resist.'

I ran upstairs and jumped into my things, then ran down again like the mouse in Hickory-Dickory-Dock. Giles gave me a farewell hug and kiss in the hall. I hugged and kissed him back.

'Good luck with your Cocker, little angel,' he said. 'But don't forget where I live.'

I let myself out into the cold street. I'd never before had such a strong sensation of wanting to be in two places at once.

SIX

There's a story called The Lady or the Tiger, which ends with a princess's young suitor having to choose to open one of two closed doors. Behind one of them sits the princess of his dreams. He will have her hand in marriage if he gets this right. Behind the other door however, a tiger sits. Get this wrong and he'll be eaten up...

OK, the parallel wasn't exact, but as I climbed the staircase to the room I shared I had the similar sensation that what greeted me when I opened the door would be the turning-point of my life. I turned the handle and pushed the door. The light was on. I went on in. Cocker was sitting up in bed in the blue and white striped pyjamas I'd now grown fond of, playing with his phone.

He turned and smiled at me. I felt good about that. I smiled at him. Perhaps a bit too fondly. I warned myself to be careful not to feel too much. And if I did feel it, then not to show it too much. If I let myself do either of those things there would be only one outcome I could be sure of. I'd end up getting hurt.

Thinking about that I almost failed to realise that I'd passed the Lady or the Tiger test. The twin tigers I'd been fearful of – Cocker's absence or Eleanor's presence – had not greeted me on my arrival in my room. Whereas Cocker had.

I could have asked him what had happened with Eleanor. He could have asked me where I'd been all evening. Neither of us did. Both questions were like unexploded hand grenades. Had either of us lobbed our one, the other would have come fizzing back. Instead we said something trite about the weather. Then I was conscious of him watching me, but trying not to look like he was, while I got undressed for bed.

'Goodnight. Sweet dreams, and dry ones,' he said when we'd put out the lights.

'You too, mate,' I said.

There was a tension in the dark room after that. We both knew the other was awake, though we were very silent. Each of us was waiting for the sounds the other made when – if – he started to masturbate. There were inferences to be drawn by both of us from whether we did or not. If Cocker didn't go for it beneath the duvet I'd draw the conclusion that he didn't need to, having had sex already with Eleanor. And if I didn't do it Cocker might guess that I'd had sex with someone else.

This went on for about ten minutes. The tension seemed almost visible in the darkness, like a guitar string, or a hawser, about to snap. I don't know to this day whether to think of Cocker as the braver one, or as the one who blinked. Because he went for it first.

I heard the movement of his duvet and his mattress as he got started. And then I had a new thought. If I let him go ahead without 'shadowing' him, so to speak – would he be embarrassed, or feel silly? Would he feel down if he thought I'd had sex with someone else and he hadn't? I didn't want him to feel down because of that. I knew I didn't need to shoot again just yet, after what had happened just an hour before. I wasn't even sure that I'd be able to, having felt, then seen, the spectacular abundance of my ejaculate. But, because I wanted to show my solidarity with Cocker, my loyalty and support – my affection, if you like – I thought I owed it to him to have a try at least.

It wasn't as difficult as I'd thought.

I heard, almost felt Cocker climax. A moment later I did the same. It seemed there was plenty to go round, for both of us.

After another minute's silence I took a risk. I whispered, 'Goodnight, Cocker.'

There was a pause. And then I heard him say, 'Goodnight, Pip.' He made a sound then that might have been a tiny giggle. I felt my heart warm me like a quick little fire. I felt my heart reach out across the dark room to Cocker. I wanted to cry. I though my chest would burst.

'Lady, shall I lie in your lap?' I said. I lay down at Eleanor's feet.

'No, my lord,' said Eleanor.'

'I mean, my head upon your lap?' I said.

Eleanor said, 'Ay, my lord.'

I answered, 'Did you think I meant *count*ry matters?'

James interrupted us. 'Pip, I don't think you need to point up the play on words quite as much as that. The audience will get Shakespeare's point quite easily enough.'

'OK,' I said. 'Point taken.' I did it again, but with a more standard inflection. 'Did you think I meant country matters?'

'I think nothing, my lord,' Eleanor said.

'That's a fair thought to lie between maids' legs,' I went on.

'What is, my lord?' she said.

'Nothing,' I said, and tweaked the toe of her shoe. That was a new thing. I hadn't thought to put it in before.

Eleanor leaned and touched my shoulder. That was new too. 'You are merry, my lord,' she said.

We looked into each other's eyes quite a lot as that intimate scene continued. It was difficult to tell what we read there, though. At least, it was for me. Maybe women really do see further and deeper than us men. But I was curious. More than curious. I wanted to know – even if the knowledge wounded me – whether Cocker had laid his head in her lap, so to speak, or whether nothing much had happened that night. That thing about him wanking afterwards proved nothing in the end, I'd realised. I thought of my own case. I'd embarked on my own wank that night as soon as he'd started his, in order, first, to make it not too obvious to Cocker that I'd recently had sex with someone else and second, out of solidarity with him, and tender feelings towards him. Cocker was at least as sensitive a boy as I was: might not his motivations for doing what he'd done in bed that night have been identical to, and as generous as, my own?

Will, the man who'd competed with me for the role of Hamlet, and ended up playing my wicked uncle Claudius, became a good friend to Cocker and to me. He bore no grudge for the fact that I'd got the part of Hamlet and he had not. I thought that was very big of him. I also thought, and Cocker thought so too, that he was brilliant in the role of Claudius. It helped that he was big and muscular, with a good handsome face, and a mop of black curls. We'd often go for a drink at The White Rabbit or the Eagle and Child after rehearsals if those were in the evening. Sometimes that would mean all of us who'd been rehearsing together that day, sometimes just Will and Cocker and me. 'You two,' Will would call us sometimes, and he'd shake his black-mop head with a wry smile on his face as though we were the source of some amusement to him. Did he think we were an item? I wondered. I loved the idea that anyone might even imagine that. By now I very much wanted it to be so. But I didn't dare to imagine the thing I would have liked to imagine: namely, that Cocker felt the same.

One evening Will broached the subject I hadn't had the temerity to raise with Cocker. 'How do you get on with our Ophelia, Eleanor?' He aimed it as a general question, something that might be answered by either of 'us two'.

Cocker picked it up. 'I took her out one evening last week,' he said. 'She was fine.' He did a sort of facial shrug. 'Nothing very much happened, if that's what you're wondering.' He addressed that to Will, looking him fair and square in the eye. But I was pretty sure he intended his answer for me alone. He was telling Will in my presence what he guessed that I rather than Will really wanted to know. The question I couldn't bring myself to ask him. The answer he couldn't bring himself to volunteer when we were on our own. It's wonderful what the presence of a helpful third party can sometimes do.

After a pause Cocker volunteered a little extra. 'We kissed,' he said. 'But that was all.'

I wondered, did you get your face slapped? As I'd had mine slapped by Cate. There was no way I'd ever ask him that, though. There are still just a few things that men have to bury till their dying day.

In bed at night the little routine that Cocker and I had tried a couple of times, the little private but not-so-private wank we each had under our own duvet shortly after we put the lights out, became a bit of an established ritual. It didn't happen every night at first. Perhaps two or three times a week. I had wanks at other times as well as that, and I had no doubt the same went for Cocker too. Struggling to write an essay, or read a boring book, alone in the room... Well, I supposed that most boys did that. But it wasn't information that Cocker and I shared between us.

But those others, the night-time ones... They became more frequent as term went on. We also became less concerned with the pretence that we wanted to do it quietly. I somehow guessed he liked to hear me thrash about and moan a bit, so I did those things. I know I liked to hear the progress he was making towards his own climax. And he obviously realised that. He took to thrashing around, scissoring his legs beneath the duvet and letting out a little cry when he came.

At some point – I don't know exactly when it was, because you can't record the moment when a routine becomes fixed – it became a nightly thing. We'd put our lights out ('Goodnight. Sweet dreams and dry ones.' 'You too.') and almost immediately both start. And afterwards there would be a little pause and one of us would say, in a quiet and intimate tone of voice, 'Goodnight, Cocker,' or 'Goodnight Pip,' depending which of us spoke first – it wasn't always the same way round: that was one of the few variable things about the scenario – and the other would reply in the same two words, and the same gentle tone. Then there'd be a little giggle, which we both shared.

Goodnight, Cocker... How I loved saying that each night. Goodnight, Pip. How I loved hearing that, whispered in reply. I wanted to amend that, though, after a few weeks had passed. *I love you, Cocker,* was what my heart wanted to whisper... I didn't dare say it out loud, of course. I'd have wanted to hear the whispered answer, *I love you, Pip.* But those words might not have been his reply. There might not have been a reply at all. I couldn't have survived my fall into the abyss of that particular silence. So I didn't dare utter those talismanic words.

Since thought is free, think what thou will,
O troubled heart, to ease thy pain.
Thought unrevealed can do no ill,
But words once past turn not again.

King James I and VI wrote that. He was gay, incidentally. He wrote those lines when he was fifteen.

When I was fifteen I was the bell-ringer in my boarding-house at school. We didn't have an automatic system. It was considered good for us to have a bit of responsibility from time to time. The bell-ringer in the other house was my friend Alex. The systems were independent. Yet there was a special button that, if you pressed it, rang a small buzzer in the other house. In case of emergencies, I suppose. After we'd pressed the final bell of the evening Alex and I had the habit of hitting this buzzer with three very quick short blips. That was my very public but also very private goodnight to Alex, and his coded goodnight to me. Goodnight, Alex. Goodnight, Pip. Three syllables each. It could have been *I love you*, though. It could have been *I love you*.

We were only fifteen, Alex and I at that time. A bit young to know precisely what the buzzes signified. A bit young to have to decide.

I came out of a late morning lecture one day and went straight into hall for lunch, carrying my books and files with me, not going up to my room to dump them first. I was quite hungry, and wanted to get on and eat. I noticed that Cocker wasn't in lunch, but I didn't give it much thought. It was fish and chips today, and they were quite nice. Cocker might be eating later, or eating somewhere else. He might have gone out to a pub with someone. We didn't live in each other's pocket, after all, so I didn't think too much about it.

I didn't even think about where Cocker might be when I climbed the stairs to our room and opened the door. But once I got inside the room I knew exactly where he was. He was curled up in bed, under his duvet, like a squirrel in a ball. There was no sign of even his head.

At least I supposed it was Cocker.

'Cocker,' I said to the rolled up bundle under the bedclothes, 'Are you all right?'

There was an unfurling movement and a head popped out near the top. It was definitely Cocker's. I was relieved about that. His face looked drawn, though. His eyes not quite their usual shiny bright. He obviously wasn't all right. 'What's the matter, mate?' I asked.

'I think I've got a chill of some sort,' the duvet-hooded face said. 'I keep having to get out of bed to piss, then when I get back in I can't warm up.'

'Oh hey,' I said. 'That's not very nice. Have you eaten anything? Taken anything? How long have you been like that?'

'It came on quickly,' he said. 'I was fine at my nine o'clock tutorial but on the way back I sort of just collapsed. I took some Paracetamol...' His father was a doctor, so that had presumably been the right thing to do. 'I don't feel like eating, though...'

I said, 'Not even if I went up to the Metro in Magdalen Street and got you a pasty or something and some packets of Cup-a-Soup?'

He wrinkled his nose a bit. 'Not right now,' he said. 'Maybe later that would be nice.'

'I'll do that as soon as you say the word,' I said. And of course I would. I'd have walked to London and got those things from Selfridge's if he'd asked me to. Barefoot. I said, 'I don't like the idea you can't get warm, though.' The obvious struck me at that moment. It struck him at the same time. I could see it expressed in a flicker of mixed and complex feelings, passing in less than a second over his face. 'Look,' I said, 'I'm going to do something about that. Whether you like it or not. No arguments please.'

I still had my jacket on. I took that off, and then my shirt. He didn't say anything. From his place of safety under the duvet he watched me undressing, with an unreadable look on his face.

I took the whole lot off. Including socks and underpants. I lifted one top corner of the duvet. He wriggled backwards away from me to give me room alongside him. I climbed in there next to him. My naked body next to his pyjama-ed one. I wondered about putting my arms around him. Maybe he'd think that was going a bit far. Even in hospitals the nurses aren't supposed to do that. But I needn't have worried, apparently. While I was still hesitating he wrapped his arms, admittedly a bit shyly, around me instead.

SEVEN

I'm wondering how I'm going to describe the rest of that afternoon. How much I should describe. How much, in order to avoid boring you, I ought to leave out. Well, we'll see how it goes, and if it turns out I've gone into things a bit too much for your taste, or left too much out … I apologise in advance.

I'd been knocked out by the embrace of Giles's muscular arms more than once a few weeks back. I'd loved the sensation I had when Alex hugged me outside the pub back in the summer, just before we both left school. And Cocker had taken me in his arms before – how would I ever forget that? – when I'd come back to our room on our second or third night as room-mates, me close to tears after my first encounter with Giles.

I'd thought Cocker was the strong one. That I was the little lost boy who'd twice run away to Giles. Cocker wasn't someone who needed me, I'd thought. But as I felt his diffident arms encircle me – his pyjama sleeves sliding back up his forearms as they came around my nakedness … It isn't easy to write, this next bit … I knew he needed me, just then, even more than I needed him.

I can't describe the feelings I discovered inside me at that point. I'm in good company there. Hemingway couldn't. Melville couldn't. Nor could Dickens, Eliot or Defoe. Maybe Shakespeare did. Maybe Dante, maybe Virgil... If they did, I haven't found the relevant paragraphs or verses. The funny thing is, dear reader, that you already know exactly what I'm on about without having to ask.

We didn't speak for ages. Just held each other. (You've already assumed, quite rightly, that once he'd put his arms tentatively around me – so tentatively that it was as if he'd feared a rebuff … how absurd! … I put my own arms around him.) I unbuttoned his pyjama top and pulled the flaps apart so that I could press the warm skin of my chest against the warm skin of his. Partly so that I could warm him up more quickly. Partly because... OK. You know.

And the loveliest thing of all was that after a little while of simply holding and being held, he drifted into sleep. I freed one of my hands and very softly stroked his lovely hair. I revelled in the unthreatening milky smell of him. I felt as though I owned him then, though not in any sinister kind of way, because it also felt – especially because his arms were round me – as though he owned me.

I undid the button of his pyjama trousers and they flopped open at the waist. I ran a finger slowly, gently down the little swirly line of hairs that joined his navel to his springy bush of pubes. I took my time, savouring every second of the journey, and then my exploring finger found his cock. Because he wasn't feeling well it was very small. I found I was deeply moved by that discovery. I stroked it a little with my forefinger and thumb. But then I stopped. I just held it quietly.

And then I must have dozed off. Because the next thing I knew was that I was still holding Cocker's small silky penis … and he was holding mine.

Was he asleep still? Had he briefly woken, grabbed me and gone back to sleep? Or had he reached out for me in his sleep? Whichever, it was a lovely compliment. I squeezed his infinitesimally. Oh wow... He did the same to mine.

I nuzzled my cheek against his cheek. He made a noise. A sort of, 'Mmmm.'

I cooed back to him in the same terms.

Then he spoke. He said, 'Sorry, but I need to get out and piss again.'

So did I, it seemed.

Cocker and I

Cocker's pyjama bottoms fell down around his ankles as soon as he got out of bed. He stepped calmly out of them. We peed companionably into the wash-basin side by side. Neither dared to touch the other's cock while we were doing that. We didn't speak, either. But at one point our eyes met and we both broke into a cautious smile. Then, still without either speaking or touching, we returned to Cocker's bed and got back in. Me naked, he with only his pyjama top on now: the bottom bit he'd left discarded on the floor.

We had to seize the moment. Delay would have snuffed out the flame, perhaps for good. I'm not talking about the flame of desire, but the flame that turns desire to deed, the flame of hot courage that's needed when you turn your back on society's expectations of you. When you turn your back on your own expectations of yourself too. I'm talking about the flame that tells you, whether you want to hear it or not, who you really are. And so I put my arms around him again and he again put his arms round me. Then I felt his hand run down my back. Cocker was taking the lead. He astonished me then by reaching down my buttock-cleft, feeling round underneath and tickling me where no-one had tickled me before: just behind my balls. 'That's nice,' I said. That was my understatement of the year to date.

He said, 'We should have done this before.'

I reached for his cock again. A watched pot never boils, but take your eye off it for a few minutes... I wanted to write, a watched cock never stiffens, but that's manifestly untrue. However, you get the point.

And so did I. What a transformation had come about during those few seconds after we'd peed together and then got back into bed. Cocker's cock was big and hard and hot now, and so was mine. As far as mine was concerned, I rather had the feeling that it had got bigger than it had ever been before.

We did exactly what we'd done at the beginning of term. We wanked each other off under the duvet, facing each other, lying on our sides. It was just the same, except that it was still afternoon and still light, and people were coming and going on the staircase outside. It was just as nice. And at the same time nicer by a multiple of infinity. Whatever doubts might assail us later, and in the days ahead, we could not, this time, file the thing under *One-offs*.

We added a bit of a refinement, though. When we'd both come I reached out of the bed and grabbed Cocker's pyjama bottoms from off the floor, and used them to wipe our wet tummies and sticky pricks. Then I chucked them back on the floor. Cocker set the alarm on his phone and we went back to sleep, nestled together again in the snugness of Cocker's warm duvet.

Before sleep came and kidnapped us I asked Cocker, 'You beginning to feel better, mate?'

'You bet your life,' he said. Had we been cats you'd have heard us both purr at that point.

Sometimes a chill can last as little as a few hours. Rest and a bit of warmth can sort it in a jiffy. When we woke up – when Cocker's phone bleeped, that was – he was restored to his usual self. He didn't even need to piss.

We got dressed. There were still about forty minutes before dinner. We looked at each other, unsure what to say at first. Then Cocker found a few words. 'Miracle cure, that's you,' he said. Then, 'Shall we have a drink in the college bar before dinner?'

'Best idea yet,' I said. We grinned at each other. It was a good idea, of course, but it was far from being the best one yet. We'd had that one earlier and acted on it. Lucky us.

It wasn't part of our usual routine, a beer before dinner. It seemed odd when we went into the bar to be greeted by people we knew. People who looked very much at home in this place at this particular time. We said hallo to various people, then ordered a half pint each at the counter. Just a half; there was a rehearsal after dinner in which we were both involved.

The trouble is, and yet it's a nice thing too, it sort of shows. A guy and a girl from my tutorial group were sitting at the next table to ours. The guy leaned towards us. 'You look very pleased with yourselves,' he said. 'What you been up to?' He hadn't really guessed, of course. Had we been of different sexes it would have been all too obvious how we'd spent the afternoon and he wouldn't have dreamed of asking the question.

'Oh, I don't know,' Cocker said. 'Rehearsals are going well. I guess that's it.' It gave me a small thrill, hearing him lie fluently like that. Cocker covering our tracks. *Our* tracks. I allowed myself to think: *us*.

At dinner we sat next to each other. The same thing happened. More than once. Cate spoke to us. I was back on easy terms with her now, although I hadn't been up to her room again and we certainly hadn't kissed. She said, 'You look like the cats that got the cream, the pair of you.'

'Do we?' I said. 'I don't know. Hamlet's coming on a treat. Maybe that's it.' The funny thing was that, although we were in fact going to say anything except the truth, we – well, I certainly, so probably Cocker too – wanted nothing more than to blurt it out. *We spent the afternoon naked in bed together. We loved being there, curled up close. We had sex too, and that was great, though oddly enough the sex was not the most important part.* Well, obviously neither of us was actually going to say that. It's a funny thing, the truth.

After dinner we trooped up Beaumont Street to rehearsals. No, not arm in arm, nor holding hands – heaven forbid! We didn't need to express our new situation in those ways just then. We had the luxury of a shared bedtime to look forward to. Whatever might happen then, whatever might not. We'd deal with it in due time. For now we were just two students going to rehearse a play, our deeper feelings pushed down for just an hour or two. Hamlet and Horatio after all were just good friends. Nothing more than that.

Time had gone whizzing along. The dress rehearsal was only days away now. Then would come our string of five performances. Perhaps because of the nearness of that climax Cocker and I were on top form at that evening's rehearsal. Well, perhaps it was because of that...

I had the feeling now that all our fellow cast members seemed to know. There's an extra dimension given to your awareness, I think, when you're on stage with someone, playing a scene with them. I saw Eleanor, and also the woman playing Gertrude, give the two of us a very searching look. Some of the others too. Nobody said anything. But...

Only three of us went for a drink afterwards. The usual suspects. Cocker and me, and Will. Will said, 'Oh let's go to The Randolph this time,' and we did.

When we got there Will coughed up for our three pints. Then when we had sat down he came out with it. 'Well, well, you two,' he said. He grinned at us like a rather big imp. 'I suppose you know it's written all over your faces.'

'What is?' Cocker said, adopting a puzzled frown.

'Oh, Cocker,' said Will, laughing. 'I do love it when you try to act!' As I've written before, Cocker didn't act. That was the beauty of his performance as Horatio. He simply brought himself to the part. 'It's plain for all the world to see,' Will went on, 'that you've got it on at last. I mean. You can still deny it if you want to...'

'Bloody hell...!' Cocker was still trying valiantly.

Will steamrollered him. '...But it's still true. About time too, I thought. And yes, I think it's great.' He chinked his pint glass against our two. 'Cheers, guys. And welcome to the club.'

I suppose I ought to have guessed that Will was gay. Somehow I hadn't spotted it. Too bound up with Cocker, I guess. Too self-absorbed by *us*.

'OK,' Cocker said. 'You win, Will. But can we please keep it between the three of us?'

Will said solemnly, 'I won't breathe a word to a single soul. I cross my heart.' And there and then, he did, drawing his forefinger down, then across his chest. He continued, 'But I can't be responsible for what others may guess. If you want to keep the thing your big dark secret ... Well, you'll have to do better – act better, I mean – than that. Learning to lie, in body language, is pretty damn difficult.'

'It's just that it's all so soon,' I bleated pathetically. 'It only happened today...'

'I know,' said Will, nodding his head gently. 'I can see that.

While Cocker, mortified, buried his face in his hands and said, 'No... Pip!'

'Sorry, Cocker,' I said miserably. 'It's just that Will seems to know everything in advance. I'm not going to go saying this in front of anyone else....'

We were released from this tangle by the entry into the bar of someone else. I couldn't see who it was, because the main door was behind me. But Will, who was facing the other way, clearly knew the person, as he looked up and smiled a welcome as they approached. 'Here's someone I know,' Will said to Cocker and me very quickly, then he turned to the new arrival and said, 'Come and join us.'

Well, I'd thought we were being released from our tangle until I turned to look at the person who'd been invited to join our table. And then I saw that the tangle had hardly started to be a tangle. The newcomer was Giles.

Will introduced us all. 'Giles. This is Giles, guys. And Giles, this is Cocker, this is Pip.'

Giles reached over and shook hands with Cocker a bit formally. 'Lovely to meet you, Cocker,' he said. Then he eye-balled me very steadily. There was a second's stand-off as we both wondered how we were going to play this. To lie or not to lie, that was the question. It was another Lady or the Tiger moment. Giles took the responsibility upon himself. 'Hi, Pip,' he said, and smiled at me. And in the most casual of asides said to the others, 'Pip and I have already met.'

Well, he might have been only an amateur thesp. like the rest of us but, blimey, Giles knew how to act.

'Oh?' said Cocker, using an inflection he'd probably never used before. Certainly I'd never heard him do it. It was the *Oh* that's used only by partners. And even then, only when they're feeling both possessive and threatened.

'Remember back at the beginning of term?' I said. I felt I had to divulge something. 'When I'd been out on my own the night you went to Freshers' Ball, and I told you I'd met someone in a pub and we'd had a drink? Well, that was Giles.'

I realised as I spoke that I should have left this to Giles. With his seniority and experience of life he might have managed to say something that closed the issue down. I, on the other hand, had opened things right up. Like I'd taken a tin-opener to a catering-size can of worms. I'd taken Cocker's mind back to that night with a single thrust.

It was the night I'd come home upset. Cocker had comforted me. He'd taken me to bed. We'd had the life-changing experience of our first mutual wank. That had crowded out the question of what had upset me in the first place. It had only once been referred to again, and then I'd just said, 'Water under the bridge.' The morning afterwards we'd agreed to bury our memory of our first night in bed together. It looked as though Cocker had buried the question … *What upset you, Pip? Before all that happened, I mean* … even deeper than that. But now I'd just come along and dug it up. I felt I was suddenly in a situation that was beyond me. Getting into bed with Cocker at last had been the easy bit, apparently. I now saw that the difficult bit was everything that had flowed, that was flowing, and that would flow from that epic moment. Life had become terribly complicated in the blink of an eye, it seemed. It was as if I'd been plucked out of my living-room and set down in the driving-seat of a London bus, full of people, and in heavy traffic, and told, 'Now drive *that*.'

'Oh right,' said Cocker, very slowly. He didn't say, *I meant to ask you about that*. At least, not in words. But his tone of voice did. And I knew that he would ask me. When we were alone together, and he judged the time was right.

EIGHT

We were alone together about an hour later, walking 'home' down Beaumont Street. The clock above the college entrance loomed and gloomed in front of us in its classical pediment. Relaxed by two pints of bitter, Cocker threw an arm carelessly around my shoulder. 'Oh fucking shit, mate,' he said.

I threw an arm around his shoulder. 'Oh fucking hell,' I said. I remembered the two boys I'd seen straggling arm in arm along the canal tow-path weeks ago. We'd become them now, it seemed. They were us.

When we were alone together, and he judged the time right... We were alone together but, thank God, Cocker did not judge the time to be right. The Giles thing would be difficult for us to handle. A ticking time-bomb, it might yet blow us apart. We didn't know what cold winds might blow on us in the morning. For the moment, for the moment … we just wanted tonight...

'Oh, fuck you mate,' Cocker said in a tone of the utmost tenderness. He even began the next bit. 'I...' He didn't do the remaining two words. Neither of us was ready for that.

I hauled his shoulder even closer into mine, wrenching us together so hard that the bones nearly smashed. 'Me too, mate,' I said. 'Oh fucking shit.'

We cleaned up our language as we came to the end of Beaumont Street and crossed the road to our front gate. We even disengaged our arms from each other's shoulder as we ducked through the open postern and entered the hallowed precincts. It would only be a minute before...

We went into our room and shut the door and turned on the light. We were all over each other in an instant. I held Cocker's ears like the two handles of a trophy cup I'd won, as I thrust my tongue down his throat. He thrust his tongue down mine. You know those narrow streets in old towns that you think should by rights be one-way streets but are not yet? Well, it was just like that.

For ages we were too busy to have time to undress. I felt every fold of his clothing and he grew intimate with every seam and crease of mine. I explored his bum-cheeks through his jeans; I hadn't got round to them before now. They were beautiful, high-worn and sculpted. They felt lovely through his clothes. I had the luxury of knowing that within minutes I'd hold them naked in my palms. I felt Cocker feeling my own buttocks up. I said, 'Oh mate. Oh fuck.'

We were two highly articulate boys, starting a degree course each. We spent our evenings steeped in the nuanced holograms of Shakespeare's deep verse. Yet that was the best we could come up with in between chewing each other's tongues. Oh mate. Oh fuck. Perhaps all of us are like that. Perhaps Shakespeare was. I did hope so. Hoped so very much.

We didn't even think of cleaning our teeth. We started to undress each other. First time we'd done that. The first time we... The marvel of first times.

'Your place or mine?' I said.

'Mine,' Cocker said. Then, in between kisses, 'My bed's kind of used to us...xxx... We've been in it most of the day...xxx... Break yours in next time.'

So we went back to what was now a very familiar and comforting place: the space between Cocker's duvet and his bottom sheet. It now looked, and felt, and probably smelt, like home.

We were getting used to each other's body now. Getting used to the way we liked to be touched and held. We were learning which bits of the other produced the most thrilling sensations when we touched them. Learning how each other's cock worked. Learning how the other came. Sharing knowledge, sharing sensation, making free gifts to each other of our sperm. We didn't do anything more advanced than what we'd done in the afternoon and at the beginning of the term. We didn't need to. We were each celebrating the capture of the other's most fugitive and indefinable essence. I'm not sure what the most straightforward word for that little lot is. It might be heart.

There were banal and commonplace things also entangled in the beauties of that wonderful night. Getting up to piss, of course. Pins and needles caused by lying on the other's arm, and having to wake him up to sort it out. And that bane of lovemaking in a single bed: muscle cramp. Those things might have been expected to take away from the solemn beauty of my first full night in bed with Cocker. But because life and beauty and fondness are more complex and mysterious things than we can begin to imagine, they did not.

I didn't return to my own bed in the small hours. We were too close now for that. We stayed together till breakfast time. Then we reluctantly got up and got dressed. We walked together through the gardens and into hall. 'I've changed my mind about something since last night,' Cocker said.

A chill blew through me. 'What?' I said, falling into an abyss.

'If people guess about us, then let them,' he said a bit gruffly. 'I'm not going to go all public about it. But Will was right about lying. There's no point.' He looked at me challengingly. 'What do you think?'

I was almost shaking with relief. 'That's what I think,' I said. 'Whatever we are, we are. Nothing else to be said.'

Cocker nodded gravely. We were converging now with other people straggling towards hall from different directions. 'Good,' he said. We walked into breakfast together and sat next to each other to eat.

I'd said, 'Whatever we are, we are: nothing else to be said,' but I was wrong there. There was a great deal else to be said. It came out in dribs and drabs over the next few days. To save my time and yours I've taken an editorial decision and telescoped it a bit.

'I've nothing against gay people,' Cocker said. 'I'm just a bit against the idea of being one myself.'

'I'd go along with that entirely,' I said. 'You've kind of taken the words out of my mouth.'

'The thing is,' he went on, 'it does kind of limit your options a bit. I mean, being straight, you've half the planet to choose from when it comes to looking for a mate. If you're gay, your field is – what – one fortieth of that?'

Where he plucked that fraction from I had no idea. But then he was studying Economics; I wasn't. No doubt he had the edge over me when it came to meaningful percentages and statistics.

'I know what you mean,' I said. 'But straight people don't actually get it on with half the people on the planet. Although in some cases they have a good crack at that. Most people settle for just a few. To try out, I suppose. Then narrow it down to just one.'

'The lucky ones do,' Cocker said.

'I guess you're right,' I said. 'It's very much a matter of luck.' We looked hard at each other then, but our eyes were not giving away very much. I might have thought of elephants and rooms just then, only we weren't in a room but walking along Beaumont Street.

The dress rehearsal was a bit of a mess; the fencing bouts we'd practised so carefully derailed themselves and got into chaos. It was a miracle none of us was killed. We all said that the chaos was a good sign. The old theatre adage goes: bad dress rehearsal, good first night.

Around this time I noticed that people I knew well or even slightly were giving me rather more than usually searching looks when we met. They'd say hallo and then their eyes would linger on me as we talked – if we talked. There was nothing hostile in those looks. There was curiosity, though, and something appraising in them. It was as though they were trying to work something out – like an equation which had too many unknowns for it to work. I told myself it was because I was about to play the Prince of Denmark in public and they were all wondering what I'd make of it.

I didn't mention any of this to Cocker. Most of our free time was taken up with the play still, and we were necessarily together for all of that. But the best moment of every day was bedtime. We'd got into a routine of sleeping in alternate beds on alternate nights. That was almost the only variable. Nothing else changed much. We sometimes undressed each other, sometimes ourselves. Then we got into bed naked and masturbated each other tenderly, finally rocking each other to sleep in our arms.

Ejaculating with Cocker, ejaculating over Cocker, Cocker ejaculating over me... That was good. More than good. But it wasn't the best bit. The best bit was *everything*. It was going to sleep together; it was waking up together; it was the sharing of our animal warmth. It was the lovely smell of Cocker, among other things, and the fact – something I'd never guessed at in advance – that we began to smell alike. I smelt like Cocker and he smelt like me. We never mentioned that to each other of course, though Cocker must have been as aware of it – and perhaps as enchanted by it – as I was.

There was a little noise we started to make. A little snicker in the throat, a little hum, through closed lips, of a laugh. Hm-hm-hm. Three syllables mostly. We'd do it as we were putting our arms around each other, arranging ourselves immediately after getting into bed. We'd do it at the moment we started work on each other's cock. (When we were actually on the brink of coming we were more articulate. Rude words and swear words and silly childish words came tumbling out, along with assorted moans and gasps.) We'd return to our hm-hm-hm noises as we drifted towards sleep. We never talked about this obviously, or allowed ourselves to analyse what the three-syllable thing might mean: we just let the sound speak for itself.

We were in the dressing-room, ready in our costumes, at the beginners' call. I wasn't included among the beginners. They were Bernardo, Francisco, Marcellus and Cocker. 'Break a leg,' I told him, standing up alongside him as he got up and turned towards the door, and touched his sleeve.

Will, who like me didn't appear till Scene 2, stayed sitting. 'You two,' he said to Cocker and me. 'Break a leg.'

'What, one leg between the pair of them?' said someone, with a laugh. And then there was a sudden silence as all round the room the penny dropped.

'I see,' said someone else, though not unkindly, and then the beginners, Cocker included, headed off out.

Will didn't try to say anything. He just looked at me with a grimace and a shrug that were half apologetic and half not. The half-not bit kind of said, *well, everybody knew anyway, didn't they?* I gave Will a smile and a shrug back.

A minute later and, via the backstage sound system we heard the play begin. My heart was in my mouth as I waited to hear Cocker's voice. Soon it came. Stalwart and strong. Clear and loud. *'Friends to this ground...*

A piece of him...

Tush, tush! 'twill not appear...

Well, sit we down, and let us hear Bernardo speak of this...'

The vigour with which he spoke the lines made my own confidence soar. Will reached across and took my hand. 'You're going to be all right.'

I said, 'You too, mate.'

And in no time at all it was our turn to walk into the wings. Our paths crossed with the actors from the first scene – including Cocker – coming off. Cocker and I passed each other. There was barely time to stop and speak. Our hands reached and brushed across each other's tummy as we nudged past. 'You're good, mate,' I said to him.

'Give it to 'em,' he said at the same moment. Then, 'Hm-hm-hm,' we both went.

My cue was in Will's lines. I breathed in deeply as he said, 'Take they fair hour, Laertes; time be thine, and thy best graces spend it at thy will. But now, my cousin Hamlet, and my son...'

Turning half away from him, I said, 'A little more than kin, and less than kind.'

'How is it that the clouds still hang on you?' Will asked.

I faced him directly. 'Not so, my lord; I am too much in the sun,' I said. We were off. An audience of hundreds of people who mostly didn't know me sat out there in the near-dark. I had emerged from the obscurity of my first few weeks at Oxford, as Hamlet, for better or worse, in the full glare of the theatre's lights.

Time rushed past. Cocker and I met on-stage, then off-stage in the dressing-room, again and again. The interval came and went. Someone brought tea round. Conversations in the dressing-room were brief, focused only on how things were going: what was good, what not so good. I felt almost that I was flying, as we got into the second half. The final act drew to its climax, in the fight scene, with death after death. There came my final scene, dying from rapier wound and poison, while Cocker crouched beside me and cradled me in his arms. My last lines came. 'I die, Horatio... The rest is silence.'

And Cocker hugged me tightly then, and rocked me – he'd never done this in rehearsal – as he said, 'Now cracks a noble heart. Good-night, sweet prince, and flights of angels sing thee to thy rest.' His voice stayed strong as he said, 'Why does the drum come hither?' But through half-closed eyelids I was watching him carefully. I saw the tears that the audience couldn't, tumbling down his cheeks.

I felt myself well up, and my chest began to heave. Cocker felt that too. He gave me a final squeeze before he laid me down and stood up for his final dialogue with the arriving Fortinbras. That was the moment at which I knew. The moment at which Cocker knew. The moment we each knew that the other knew. We had fallen in love.

NINE

We went to a club. Well, most of us did. Turned out it was only a stone's throw from our own college. There were guys dancing together on the dance-floor, some just companionably, others cheek to cheek. Cocker and I looked at each other and microscopically shook our heads. Nobody else would have seen the movement, however hard they'd looked. But even that infinitesimal signal was superfluous. We knew, as if we were one person, that we weren't going to dance. Not here. Not in public. Not tonight. There was too much that was too important between us. Some of it had only come into being tonight.

Will joined 'us two' near the bar. With him were Giles and the young man I'd seen him with at The Randolph all those weeks ago when I'd gone there with Cate. He hadn't been mentioned when I'd seen Giles a day or two later, and I hadn't seen him since. Giles said to me straight away, 'I saw the show tonight. I'll be totally serious for a moment. Your Hamlet was really great. I daren't tell you you ought to be a professional, since most actors spend most of their time out of work. Only that you could be a professional if you were stupid enough to want to be. You're that good.' He turned to Cocker. 'And you were just splendid. Everything that Horatio should be, you were. As for the rapport between the two of you...' He shrugged. 'I think I'll leave it at that.' And, bless him, he did.

He introduced his friend. He was a sweet and charming chap called Mick. I wondered if he knew about Giles and me. If he knew I'd been to Giles's house. Well, he either did or didn't. I wasn't going to bring it up.

But I was on edge now about being in the same place as both Cocker and Giles. It had been fine that last time at The Randolph. We'd all chatted together about general, safe things. But there had still been that initial proprietorial 'Oh' of Cocker's, that he'd uttered when he'd heard which night it was that Giles and I had first met. He still hadn't brought the subject up – too many wonderful things had been happening to us – but I knew he would bring it up, and now I was afraid it might be tonight.

Cocker and I stayed long enough for a few drinks, but once we'd basked in some very enjoyable adulation we got fidgety and wanted to be alone together – like a couple on honeymoon. We didn't make a pantomime of leaving separately: we'd outgrown our need to do things like that. Some people would notice us leaving together, most would not. It didn't matter. Giles gave me his card as we got up to go. He spoke to both of us. 'Come and have a drink at my place any time,' he said. He looked at Cocker. 'Just round the corner from your college.' He cleverly left it open as to whether I'd already been there or not. For all he knew I might have already told Cocker about it but, if not, it wasn't going to be through Giles that Cocker found out.

Outside, the December air gave us a shrill shock. Cocker turned to face me on the pavement. 'What do we want to do now?' he asked.

'You mean, apart from *that*.'

He chuckled. 'I mean, as well as that.'

I said, 'We could go for a short walk before bed. I mean, if you'd like.'

'Short one,' he said, 'but yeah, let's do that.' We walked along the High, then turned down Magpie Lane, past Merton, and came out into the Meadows by Dead Man's Walk. The walks that criss-crossed the meadows were lit by lamp posts, rather widely spaced. Each one was crowned with a little aura of glowing river mist. We strolled across the damp grass towards the lights and trees of the avenue that was the Broad Walk. Then Cocker came out with it. 'Have you been to his house?'

'Whose?'

'Don't pretend. Giles's.'

'Sorry,' I said. 'No pretending between us. Yes, I have. Twice.'

'You never told me about it,' said Cocker.

I said, 'You never asked.' Oh dear, I thought. Cocker didn't say anything. He clearly wanted to hear more from me first. 'OK,' I started. 'Both times were back at the beginning of term. Not recently. I didn't tell you because... because we didn't know each other so well back then.'

'You'd been there that time you came back all upset after I'd been to the Freshers' Ball. That right?'

'Yes,' I said.

'And you were about to tell me about it then – however little you knew me – but you didn't.'

'That's right,' I said. 'I didn't tell you about it because something wonderful happened. You took me in your arms, remember, and a little time after that we got into your bed. I didn't need to tell you about it because I was no longer upset.' I reached for his hand and clasped it. He was happy to hold mine. In the darkness we continued to walk over the grass like that.

'And the second time?' I felt his fingers tighten on mine just a little, involuntarily, as he asked.

'It was the night you went out with Eleanor,' I said. I hoped he'd understand all the complex stuff behind that, without my having to explain it.

He didn't ask me to explain it. He said, 'What happened each time?' instead.

We'd reached the Broad Walk and turned left towards the river. I told him the story of the first time. 'I was feeling homesick and a bit lonely. You'd gone to the ball...'

'Oh mate,' he said. In a sudden rush of emotion he caught hold of me and kissed me fiercely on the lips. Then he let me go. 'Cinderella,' he said.

I told him how Giles had come along and taken me to The Head of the River, then home to his place. That I'd cried a bit and that he'd held me. 'We felt each other up a bit,' I admitted. I told him how we'd hung on opposite sides of the door-frame, and had briefly got our cocks out. 'But I'd wanted to get back to you, actually,' I said. 'It was the same the second time. But that time Giles knew that.'

'So what happened the second time?' Cocker asked. He'd cooled noticeably since that sudden rush, a few seconds ago, into a kiss.

'The night you went out with Elsinore – I mean Eleanor.' Again I hoped the circumstances and my jealousy didn't need spelling out. He just nodded, so presumably they did not. 'I just went and knocked on his door and he let me in.'

'Is that what gay blokes do?' Cocker said coldly.

I went cold myself. My young blood froze, as Hamlet senior's ghost had warned me it might. 'I couldn't say,' I said. 'Look, I don't fucking know,' I said. 'I've no experience of being gay. It's just … that I've got you.' My voice tailed away weakly.

Cocker said, more gently. 'And I don't know either. Sorry, mate.'

'Again I needed comforting. We went upstairs and got undressed. OK, if you must know, I lay on top of him and came on his tummy. Then he wanked himself off. I didn't feel particularly bad about it, and I didn't feel particularly good. I didn't feel disloyal to you. We hadn't got to where we are now, back then. And anyway, you were spending the evening with a girl...'

'You need to stop now,' Cocker said faintly. 'I'm feeling a bit sick.'

There was nothing I could have said that would get us out of this. I turned towards him and threw my arms around him with all my strength. I was terribly afraid he'd rebuff me and fight me off. But he did not. He hugged me back so fiercely that we both tumbled down and crashed into the wet grass. It was shockingly cold, like the sea in springtime. But no other conclusion to that conversation could have been better than this.

We cuddled and tussled a bit as we rolled in the grass that was so cold, dark and wet. We squeezed each other's semi-erect penises through our jeans but felt no immediate urge to take them out. After a few moments' uncertainty, and the feeling we'd been thrown out of a space capsule and were hurtling through nothingness, we were together again and safe. In a few minutes we'd be in our safest of havens: our bedroom, and Cocker's (it was his turn to play host this evening) bed.

We got up and walked the last few yards towards the river, then turned left along the path that follows it to Magdalen Bridge. The water bubbled along beside us like an accompaniment in a song by Schubert.

I wanted to say all sorts of things about the Giles business. About how there was no question of unfaithfulness, since what had taken place had done so long before anything had really started between Cocker and me... Fortunately I found the good sense not to do that. Perhaps – actually though, almost certainly – Cocker was biting back words too.

I've quoted this before, but here it is again, from the pen of King James I and VI.

Since thought is free, think what thou will,
O troubled heart, to ease thy pain.
Thought unrevealed can do no ill,
But words once past turn not again.

King James was not a backward fifteen-year-old. The second half of that poem goes like this:

Be careful, aye, for to invent
The way to get thine own intent.
With patience then see thou attend,
And hope to vanquish in the end.

I'd often wondered what he'd been thinking about when he penned those lines. The thorny thickets of the Scottish political scenery at the time? (It was the 1590s, and everything was in flux, and deadly dangerous, during his long minority, after the execution of his mother, Mary Queen of Scots.) Or was he thinking about some boy he'd set his heart on?

I know I was.

We reached the steps that lead up onto Magdalen Bridge, where the river becomes a bobbing carpet of end-to-end, side-by-side punts laid up overnight. Above us was the road that quickly becomes the High. Even at this time of night – it was nearly two o'clock – people were walking across the bridge from time to time. Oxford is a student town, and some students never sleep.

I knew that neither of us wanted to go up there just yet. But it was Cocker this time who shamed the devil and, with a pull on my arm, told the truth. 'Just stay a sec,' he said.

I'd have happily stayed in the cold under the arch of Magdalen Bridge with Cocker until I turned into a troll, or until morning – whichever happened first.

'I just wanted to say,' he said, very quickly, nervously, 'that your Hamlet's wonderful. I can't imagine anyone ever doing it better than that. I thought you were lovely. From beginning to end.' His voice was losing its measure. There was urgency in it, and things that sounded a bit like panic and pain.

'I thought you were wonderful,' I said. I heard my own voice shake, like a car suddenly forced off-road at high speed.

He grabbed the sleeves of my jacket. 'It wasn't only that.'

'I know,' I said. 'I know what happened when you came to...' I wanted to say, *when you came to the goodnight sweet prince bit, the flights of angels bit*, but couldn't get the words out. I just saw Cocker nodding his head like crazy. I chucked my arms around his shoulders and buried my head in his neck. 'I fucking love you, Cocker.'

'Oh shit, man,' he said quietly but urgently in my ear. 'I fucking love you too, mate.'

We stood holding onto each other for ages, in the darkness of the bridge, just out of reach of the thrown light from the lamps in the street above. I thought I wanted to stay like that for ever. Except to my parents and the occasional dog or guinea-pig I'd never said *I love you* to anyone. I hadn't quite bargained for the effect it would have. You know there's a bit of a mountain on one of the Canary Islands that, when it one day falls off into the Atlantic, will create a tidal wave that floods America's eastern seaboard, destroys New York and changes the world for ever? I learned that night that those three words, *I love you,* can have a similar effect.

'I like it that we're here doing this, saying this,' Cocker said, tugging at my arms. He seemed to be talking wildly, the way half the characters in Hamlet do, as they go mad one by one. I liked it that way.

I said, not caring what I meant or what Cocker would understand from it, 'I don't want anything but this.' I only knew that this moment under Magdalen Bridge in a cone of cold darkness between two light-throws from above was the high point of my life to date.

We stayed and kissed until I felt my joints seizing with the cold, and no doubt so did my friend. As the moments passed and the cold bit deeper I found myself learning what it would be like to be thirty, then forty, then fifty... I didn't make it to sixty. Cocker whispered in my ear – he was cheek to cheek with me and stroking my hair – 'Let's go home, mate.'

We ran up the steps together. We ran down the High. From time to time one of us would swarm up a lamp-post and then drop down, to be caught in the other's arms as he fell. The shock of that impact would propel us both down onto the pavement. We sprawled on our backs, pretending to be dead ants or capsized tortoises. We played those early childhood games that in this moment weirdly came back to us. We got our cocks out and pissed in unison on the plate-glass window of a shop.

Turned right into the Corn, left into Beaumont Street, and then it was a straight line to … well, what the hell was it, this place where Cocker and I lived? This college, this muddle of buildings that dated from the middle ages, the eighteenth century and the twentieth, thanks to the generosity of Lord Everyone-knew-who...? Cocker had found a word for it. It wasn't something I'd expected at the beginning of term. Certainly not on that night when I'd stood on Folly Bridge and met Giles. Cocker's word – my word now, because everything of Cocker's was mine now – was *home*.

TEN

Oxford felt different next morning. It was different. It was as if I'd cast off the cloak of invisibility in which I'd walked the streets of the town for the past two months. Everybody who passed me in the street gave me either a cheery wave, or a *Hi, liked your Hamlet*, or at the very least a smile of recognition. I looked idly at the newspapers in the window of a newsagent's and almost jumped out of my skin. There, looking back at me, was a picture of myself, dressed as Hamlet, on the front page of the Oxford Mail. Yes, I remembered the photo-call, and the picture being taken, a couple of weeks ago. Since then I hadn't given it another thought.

I went in and bought a copy, of course. Well, you do. I handed it to the girl – I mean, woman – at the check-out, trying to look as unlike myself as possible, and not looking her full in the eye. She said, 'Nice picture of you. And the review inside's good too.'

'Oh wow,' I said, and found myself giving an embarrassed but not unhappy giggle as I briefly met her eyes.

The review was a cracker. I won't quote it in full. I sat on the nearest bench I could find in the street and read it through. I could hardly believe it. It praised the ensemble of the company, and then devoted nearly three-quarters of the rest of its column-inches to my performance. All of it was good. Better than good, actually. Better by far. It was so good, and there was so much of it, that I glanced quickly at the name of the person who wrote it. I was relieved to find it was no-one I knew. I also began to worry about squaring this with Cocker... And then I came to the last paragraph. *Special mention should be made of Cocker Davis's Horatio. A perfect foil to Rogers's Hamlet. The deep affection between the two of them is palpable. Davis is another newcomer to be watched. As the play closed he had not just Hamlet at his feet but Oxford too.* Cocker would have no cause to be envious of the praise that had been heaped on me after he'd read that. I couldn't wait to see him in an hour or two – he was in a tutorial right now – and give him the news. Meanwhile I walked back along the High, smiling at, and saying good morning to, everyone I passed, whether they had a clue who I was or not.

Cocker hadn't seen the review, nor had anyone yet mentioned it to him. I showed it to him as soon as he came back to our room from his tutorial and he was as thrilled by it as I was. The lovely thing was that he seemed as delighted by the praises that were lavished on me as by what had been written about him. Spontaneously we did a little dance together in the middle of the room. It was the dance we hadn't wanted to have in public at the club the previous night.

Cocker said, 'I don't feel like doing any more work today. Shall we go out for lunch?'

I didn't feel like doing any more work that day either. I said I thought his was a good idea. There was a riverside walk that everyone knew about but that we had never done. It started from just beyond the station, and followed the snaking Thames (or Isis) through Port Meadow for about three miles. It ended up, via Godstow weir, at the very famous Trout Inn.

It would have been enchanting in the summer. We had that still to come. Actually we had three of them still to come. Even in December though, with rime or hoar-frost silvering trees and meadow and the low sun peering through the whitened branches overhead, it was lovely enough. As we walked away from the city centre, so the city receded and became a picture: the one everybody is familiar with. That honey-coloured skyline: a surging up of dreaming domes and towers and spires.

It wasn't the beauty of the walk itself that was best though. It was the beauty of the boy walking beside me. Boy. Man. It doesn't matter which of those he was. Nor did it matter that he wasn't beautiful in the way the men who model for Armani and Hugo Boss are beautiful. He was just Cocker, my Cocker, and for me that was beauty enough.

The approach to The Trout was charming, mind you. Via a little lane, over two hump-back bridges made of ancient Cotswold stone. The inn itself a solid little stone building, with a roof of uneven stone tiles, overhung with trees. We were hungry when we got to The Trout, and ready for a pint. Actually we had two of those with our meal, under the light oak beams. And then we walked back home again, along the riverside. At one point a kingfisher darted in front of us like a flying blue jewel. I'd seen kingfishers before, on Exmoor, but this was the first one Cocker had ever seen. After we'd seen it and talked about it he gave me his hand to hold and we walked along for quite a way – since no-one passed us for a bit – with hands clasped.

It was gone three o'clock by the time we got back to college, and it was already dusk. It would be dark in half an hour. Then there we were, arriving back in our room, having decided to do no more work today, and with dinner still four hours away, and Hamlet's second performance after that. Cocker announced suddenly that he wanted to have a shower. 'Fine,' I said. 'I might have one after that.'

'Or else...' I could see an idea forming in his mind. 'Care to join me?' he asked.

It was the best, the soapiest and soppiest, the warmest, loveliest and cuddliest shower I'd had in my life. We were both stiff by the end of it, of course.

We ran back naked, truncheoned, into the bedroom. 'Don't get dressed,' said Cocker. 'Let's just go to bed.'

I didn't argue. Cocker was simply telling me where I belonged. But he hadn't told me that he'd formed a clear idea of what he wanted to do. Once under the duvet he pounced on top of me and rolled me on my back. 'This what you did with Giles, right?' he said.

I said, 'Yes.'

He'd brought some lotion back with him from the bathroom, and now he rubbed it in between us, coating our two tummies and our dicks. Then he started to do exactly what I'd done on top of Giles, rubbing his cock back and forth against mine and against my belly, powering it with little thrusts – which gradually grew bigger – of his hips. 'This is nice,' he said.

'Cocker,' I said. I was aware the question I was going to ask him was very intimate. 'Have you ever fucked anyone? Of either sex?'

'No,' he said. He sounded slightly ashamed of that admission, but neither my question nor his answer had any impact on the rhythm of his thrusts. He went on humping steadily. 'Have you?'

'No,' I said. 'And I've never been fucked.'

'Well, no,' Cocker said, sounding a bit taken aback. 'I guess you wouldn't have been. I mean, I haven't.'

I said, 'Is that a thing you'd like to try one day? I mean, one day with us?'

'I don't know,' he said, sounding a bit uncomfortable. 'I hadn't thought about it.'

'I hadn't though about it either till just now,' I said.

'It's a bit of a gay thing, though, isn't it?' Cocker said.

I thought for a moment. 'Isn't there something a little bit gay about us?' I prompted.

'I'm still dealing with that,' Cocker said, now squirming around on top of me in a growing thrill of delight. I thought, we've already admitted we love each other, and here we are in bed together doing this, and still we have a problem with a word of three letters. 'Me too,' I said. Sticks and stones may break my bones but names'll never hurt me. How wrong that last bit was, I thought. 'Anyway, we'll forget about the fucking bit.'

It wasn't going to be an issue right now anyway, I realised. Cocker's squirms grew more snakelike, and he said, 'Oh hey, I'm going to shoot,' which was information I was receiving already anyway. And then he did. And to my surprise I followed suit almost instantly. It had crept up on me without my noticing, and then there it was, pumping out, my semen joining Cocker's as it ran between our chests.

'We might need another shower before dinner,' Cocker said. But we didn't for the moment. We stayed where we were, cuddling warmly and wetly, for what remained of that afternoon, in Cocker's bed.

There was a custom at our college – though it was a custom more honoured in the breach than in the observance – of greeting anyone arriving for dinner who had been 'in the news' recently with an orchestrated chorus of whatever that news might be. For instance, if a guy had scored an exceptional number of goals in football, that number would be shouted out by a large section of the college when he entered the room, and the greeting would be followed by a drumming on the tables of several hundred knife handles. It had only happened twice since the beginning of term. Once to the man who had scored the record number of goals, and once to someone who had been repeatedly reprimanded on the score of overdue library books. He was welcomed with a shouted chorus of, 'Return your library books!' and a lot of friendly laughter.

This night, as Cocker and I entered hall together, it happened to us. A ragged shout arose, though it was clear enough to hear the words. They were a quote from that morning's Oxford Mail. 'Palpabale affection!

Affection palpable!' Then the laughter, and the drumming of the knives.

I was appalled. I felt my blood run cold, and drain from my face. The laughter was pretty ribald, though whether it was kindly or hostile I couldn't yet guess. It was bad enough that the incident had occurred. That someone had thought to do it, and then set up the 'pass it on' whisper around the entire hall…

For a second I didn't know what to do. Didn't know how to react. I didn't dare turn and look at Cocker. But then I heard his voice, loud, clear and un-intimidated. 'Tickets for Hamlet tonight still available from the box office. Just a few left.' There was almost a laugh in his voice as he said it. And his announcement was greeted then with a laugh from the whole hall. And applause. And a few friendly whoops. I found my face had cracked into a smile and that I'd raised my hand in a high triumphal wave for just a second. Then we walked on towards our table, and two people budged apart a little, to make room for the two of us to sit next to each other. That was the best bit.

But I had the feeling, and it persisted afterwards, that the incident could easily have gone the other way and turned nasty, and that it was Cocker who had saved it. I'd heard of people being 'outed' by the press. Now I knew what it was like.

The show went even better that second night. Normally it goes the other way, as the adrenalin that fuels the opening night is not there in quite such abundance. But the positive reaction from the newspaper had inspired all of us, and sharpened the appetite of our audience. While Cocker and I were still feeling the effects of the adrenalin that had pumped through us in that epic moment at the beginning of dinner.

Neither of us cried at the end of the play. Unlike the previous night. But Cocker cradled me even more warmly in his arms as my character breathed his last. We had one drink only in the bar afterwards, and then Cocker and I went home to bed. I thought of that last phrase, turning it over in my mind, as we walked along Beaumont Street. To have even thought the idea *Cocker and I are going home to bed* at the beginning of term would have been impossible. Impossible to imagine. Impossible to think. I said all this to Cocker. He said, 'That's amazing. Because I was just thinking exactly the same thought. In the same words. Home and bed. They've kind of become the same place for us.'

It was lovely that Cocker had had the same thought that I had. But a little cloud hung on me suddenly. We were still only just eighteen. We had three years, less a couple of months, still to go at Oxford. And then the rest of our lives. Everything was wonderful between us, and yet it was all so new and so untested. How could we – did we expect to – did we want to – make it last? 'Are we peaking too soon?' I said.

'Like, you mean, it's all so good but so new and fragile? Is that it?'

Careless as to whether anyone saw us I gave his hand a squeeze. 'You've thought my thoughts,' I said. 'In the exact same words.'

'It's like we've launched a boat, isn't it?' said Cocker. 'And we don't know what's going to happen. But we had to launch it anyway, and hope for the best. We never had a choice.'

I said, 'We sail it down the river. We can only guess what happens when we meet the open sea.'

'Exactly,' Cocker said. And I remembered the same image had come to my mind when we auditioned, and I didn't know if Cocker would be any good. I'd heard him navigating the easy waters of his dialogue with me and

Marcellus, and then I'd listened as he sailed out into the bigger challenge – even then I'd thought of it as the open sea – that was the speech that followed.

Two nights together had these gentlemen,
Marcellus and Bernardo on their watch,
In the dead vast and middle of the night,
Been thus encountered: a figure like your father,
Armed at points exactly, cap-a-pe,
Appears before them...

He'd gone bravely on into the currents of the words, the waves of thoughts, and ended perfectly:

... I knew your father;
These hands are not more like.

He had held his hands out instinctively as he said those last words: his palms upward, fingers spread, despite the script he was carrying in one of them, towards me. He'd sailed that speech magnificently that first time. He'd done so throughout rehearsals, and was now doing it in performance night after night. I hadn't dared to expect it of him in advance, and yet it had turned out that he could do it and was doing it. Maybe the same could be hoped, at least hoped, for that frail untested craft that was our relationship. Relation-*ship,* you note.

'We can but hope,' I said, and pecked him boldly on the cheek as we walked down the street.

'Do more than hope,' he said. 'We can enjoy the ride. Long may it last.' He pecked me back.

As we got to the door of our room something must have caught my eye, because I found it drawn to the little card on our door that had our names on. Cocker had arrived first, you'll remember, I second. For that reason it had always read:

Cocker Davis
Pip Rogers

But as I looked at it now I saw the order had been changed, though the writing was still ours.

Pip Rogers
Cocker Davis
'Oh fuck,' I said and pointed. 'Look at that.'

We both looked closely to see how it had been done. Very easily, of course. Someone had removed the card, cut it in two with a pair of scissors and replaced it the other way round. At least they'd left me with the dignity of a capital R for Rogers. Even so, it wasn't very nice.

'I mean, a joke's a joke,' said Cocker, once again voicing my own exact thoughts, 'but that's going a bit far. They wouldn't do it if we were boy and girl.' He sighed a bit sadly. 'I wonder who it was.' It was the easiest thing in the world, though, to put right. We took the two half cards out and put them back together the way they'd been before, attaching them together with Selotape. OK, someone could easily change them back again, but they'd need to come provided with scissors again to cut the Selotape. We didn't think anyone would go to as much trouble as that.

'Anyway,' said Cocker, 'You don't roger me. Not in the full sense of the word. Nor I you.'

I thought he was splitting hairs a bit. We'd got quite close to it with our tummy-rub that afternoon. I didn't challenge him, though. I wasn't sure, either, if I wanted to go quite that far with Cocker. It did seem to be a point of no return on the way to that three-letter word of classification we didn't want to label ourselves with.

ELEVEN

After the final performance of Hamlet there was a party in the rooms that James had in Sheridan College in the Broad – the Broad being Oxford-speak for Broad Street.

As a final year student, James was privileged to have two rooms, one for sleeping in, the other for working. It was an advantage to be a final year student when it came to party time.

We blokes stood about with cans of beer at first, while the girls sipped things like Bacardi and Coke. Eleanor seemed to have taken a renewed interest in Cocker. She must have known how the land lay between him and me. All the boys in the boys' dressing-rooms were clued up about it and, although Cocker and I didn't actually talk about our relationship in public, they would come out with the occasional good-natured joke at our expense. It was inconceivable that they didn't talk about us when we weren't there, because all of us do that, and equally impossible that they hadn't talked to the girls too. Perhaps Eleanor was simply determined to have one last try for Cocker before the end of Hamlet socialising put an end to easy access to him. She wasn't in our college, so wouldn't casually run into him there, nor was she studying his subject: Economics.

Melanie came up to me. You don't know Melanie yet. She had been playing Gertude, the Queen of Denmark, who was my mother, though Melanie, being a student herself, was no more than two years older than I was. She had wonderful blonde hair that she wore very long. 'I hope you're proud of yourself,' she said. 'Because you should be. Carrying off Hamlet in your first term.'

'Oh, hey, you're nice. But your Gertrude was pretty special too...'

She waved the hand she wasn't holding her drink in. 'It's not the same thing at all. It's my third year, for one thing, and the play's all about Hamlet, not the Queen. Are you thinking of becoming a professional?'

'Oh, I don't think so,' I said. Although of course I was. Beginning to think about it, at any rate. Certainly since that wonderful review had come out.

'Well, you could, you know. You ought to think about it at least.'

'I don't know,' I said.

Then she changed the subject suddenly. 'How are you going to deal with Christmas?'

'In what way?' I asked, feeling my forehead pinch with puzzlement.

'I mean you and Cocker. Your first time apart.'

'Oh God,' I said. 'Are people talking about that? I've hardly given Christmas a thought yet.' That was true. That Cocker and I would in a few days' time be separated by several hundred miles for a period of weeks hadn't crossed my mind. It crossed it now with a bit of a sickening lurch.

'I'm sorry if I'm being nosey,' Melanie said. 'That wasn't very tactful of me...'

I said, 'That's quite all right. It's only that I hadn't got there yet. But it's time I woke up to it. You're right.'

'Perhaps you can find some time to be together over the vac,' she said. 'Where do you both live?'

'I live on Exmoor,' I said. (I liked to see the surprised reaction of people when I put it like that.) 'Cocker's from Tunbridge Wells. They're a long way apart.'

'Oh I don't know,' she said. 'I'm sure you'll find a way to meet up.'

About a beer and a half later Will spoke to me. 'I've just heard what happened at your college dinner,' he said.

'Oh no,' I said. 'Who told you?'

'Oh, everyone's talking about it,' he said. 'There aren't Chinese walls between the colleges.' That was something I hadn't reckoned with. I'd rather stupidly imagined that if Cocker and I didn't blab, knowledge of the incident would remain limited to the several hundred members of our own college. He grinned and clapped a hand on my shoulder. 'Don't worry about it. People are cool with gayness and gay people at uni these days. It's Oxford, not Teheran.'

'Or even Moscow,' I said. 'For which one must be grateful. But there's something else, which you don't know.' A doubt flickered inside me. 'Or if you do know, tell me.' I told him about the reversal of our names on the outside of our door.

Will laughed. 'That's quite funny actually. But, no, that's not all around the university. Or if it is, I hadn't heard. Pip rogers Cocker Davis. Why did I never think of that? It's no more than the truth, I suppose.'

I heard myself saying – or rather, I heard the beer I'd drunk saying, 'Actually we don't fuck each other. We kind of do everything else, but not that.'

'Nothing wrong with that,' Will said. 'And I didn't mean to pry. Try it when you're ready. When you're comfortable with the idea.'

I said, 'Do you fuck with guys?'

'Yes,' he said, and for the first time since I'd met him I heard a hint of bashfulness in his voice.

'Which way round?' I asked. I felt a bit of a thrill run through me. I realised it was now me doing the prying.

'Both ways,' he said. 'Though I didn't do it till my second year here. I did all the other stuff that you do up till then.' He paused for a second, and gave a half smile. 'You might be interested to know that it was with your friend Giles that first time. Both ways round – before you ask me – on the same night.'

A thought shook me. 'You won't tell Giles what I just told you, will you? Please. And please don't tell anyone else.'

'I promise, Pip,' Will said. With the kind of smile that novelists describe as fond.

'It's just that Giles might...'

'Yes,' said Will. 'If he knew, he might. But he won't know – unless one of you two tells him. And by the way, I'd quite like it if you didn't tell anyone what I just told you. About my second year, and Giles and all that.'

'I promise too, Will,' I said.

'Though there's one exception on my side,' he said unexpectedly. 'You can tell Cocker if you want. I mean, only if you want to. When you think the moment's right.'

A minute later Cocker had joined us. 'Everybody seems to be talking about us,' he said.

'As I've just been discovering,' I said. I looked at him minutely. 'Are you feeling OK about that?'

'Not sure,' he said, and his eyes dipped for a second. That had never happened when he was talking to me before.

'Me too,' I said and, although we were in a social situation with other people present, I took his hand, leaned in to him and gave him a kiss as brief as a blink.

Will piped up at that point. 'Know what Oscar Wilde said? I mean, about being talked about.'

'No,' we both said.

'There's only one thing worse than being talked about – and that's *not* being talked about.'

'I guess he had a point,' Cocker conceded, and I added, 'I guess he did.' I was looking at Will, though, and found I couldn't help trying to visualise him being rogered by another bloke. He was a big, handsome strapping guy. Absolutely right for the muscular physicality and authoritative presence of Claudius. It was difficult to imagine him in the submissive role of a young man being fucked. There was a lot of food for thought in that.

Cocker and I

Towards the end of the party, some time during the small hours it struck everyone almost at the same moment that Hamlet was behind us. The great piece of theatre that had taken over all our lives – and especially mine – since the beginning of term, was a part of us all that we would never see again. The realisation was like the chiming of the clock, gentle but powerful, inexpressibly poignant, that signals the end of the ball in a piece of music I'd heard. I couldn't remember what the piece was.

Some of the women began to embrace each other and cry, and one or two of the men did likewise. I hoped that Cocker and I would not find ourselves blubbing, and was relieved that in the end we did not. Perhaps because more was beginning for us than was ending tonight.

How did the party end for the two of us? As by now you might expect. It ended with Cocker emptying his plastic cup of beer and turning to me and saying, 'We're done here, aren't we?' At which I nodded. His cue to finish, 'Let's go home, mate.'

So busy with Hamlet we were, and so busy with 'us two', that we'd hardly given a thought to the coming end of term. We hadn't registered Christmas. Suddenly there those things were. Christmas had been in the shops, apparently, since the beginning of term back in October. We hadn't noticed that.

I was an only child. I bought Christmas presents for my parents only: no-one else. I'd never had a girlfriend, let alone a boyfriend. Suddenly I found myself wondering, was I supposed to get a present for Cocker? Was he supposed to get one for me? I didn't know what to do about this. I emailed Alex.

I got a sort of boyfiend. Really want to talk to you at Xmas bout that. Dont no if I should buy him a present for Xmas tho. Need yr thoughts on this.

He emailed me back.

Did you forget the r in boyfriend, or is a boyfiend what you got? I got one too. Wd like to talk to u bout that at Xmas too. Re presents, talk to him. He's asking himself same question. Decide together what you want to do. Luv Alexxxxx

I was startled by the number of xxxs at the end of his name, and even more by the fact that Alex had a friend or fiend in the same way that I did. Incredible what happens to your mates when they go off to university and you're apart for just a few weeks. But I took Alex's advice. I put the question to Cocker under the duvet, after we'd both just come one night. 'What do we do about Christmas presents? I mean, you and me. Do we do something or just forget about it?'

'I've been thinking about it too,' he said. 'I text a friend. He said, do nothing. Save it for beginning of next term.'

I thought that good advice. But my head was spinning. Who was this male friend he was texting? He'd never told me about him. Not that I'd told Cocker about Alex, of course. I parked all that for the moment. 'What about cards?' I said.

'We can send each other those,' he said very smoothly, as if he'd been thinking about this, 'care of our parents' addresses.' I realised then that, although we had each other's phone and email, we'd never done the postcode bit.

'Do you mind if we don't get out of bed and write them down at this precise moment?' I said.

'We'll do it first thing in the morning,' he said, again very smoothly, as though he'd pre-planned even that.

'I love you, Cockerfuckercocker,' I said.

'I love you Cockerfuckerpip.' There was probably quite a lot of Freudian stuff in that goodnight valediction but we didn't think about it. We went to sleep instead.

We went to London on the same train. How wondrous strange this was. Goring and Streatley passed beside us outside the window. And Pangbourne, green hillsides among the looping coils of the Thames. We'd never been further together than Godstow, on our three-mile walk to The Trout. Now sixty miles of England were passing around us. And inside it all … we were just us.

Nearer and nearer the stations come. The names of un-stopped-at stations, whizzing past, toll the knell of the term departed, and herald a parting the like of which neither of us has experienced before. Countdown to separation at Paddington (zero hour). Reading. (Thirteen.) Twyford. (Twelve.) Maidenhead. (Eleven.) Planes clamber into the sky from Heathrow to our right now. Slough (ten), Iver (nine), West Drayton (eight). We've passed the airport: the planes are landing from the east. Hayes and Harlington (seven), Southall (six), Hanwell (five), West Ealing (four), Ealing Broadway (three), Acton Main Line. (Two.) The North Pole Eurostar depot and carriage sheds. Royal Oak. (One.) Brakes on now. Paddington, where a certain bear was lost, then found. And where we stop and part.

'I stay here,' I say. 'Find the train for Exeter.'

'And I'm on the tube for Charing Cross,' says Cocker. We know all that already. We've exchanged that information a hundred times. Now we are just saying it. Because... Well, just because.

We slip our tickets through the automatic barrier and are out on the hectic cold concourse. 'I love you and leave you here,' Cocker says.

I walk with him to the top of the escalator. We touch each other on the shoulder but don't try to kiss.

And then the escalator swallows him. It takes him down. He turns back and looks at me, like the soldier in the Houseman poem. He's beyond smiling. He just looks.

If I ever do get back,
Will you still be there?
Motionless,
At the top of the subway?
With your eyes full of me,
And your backpack
Full of paper books?

TWELVE

The incredible silence of that first day back at my parents' house. I'd never known a silence like it. My parents went to work and I was left alone in the house. The house was a big Victorian affair that had once been a farmhouse. It was situated halfway along a track that led to another farmhouse. Apart from that there was no habitation in sight. We lived among rolling hills that were clad with purple heather for most of the year. In December, though, they were just grey and dank. I've referred to the place as my parents' house. I'd thought of it as home until recently, and been homesick for it at the beginning of term. But it wasn't home any more. Home was wherever Cocker was.

I stayed in bed long after Mum and Dad had gone to work. I masturbated, of course. I thought about Cocker while I was doing that. No surprises there. But what after that? I lay in bed, festooned with fronds of cooling spunk. That sort of thing had been nice with Cocker. Alone, it was anything but. I listened for sounds about me. I heard only the whoosh of my blood in my ears and the steady rhythm of my heart. Eventually I got up. I didn't know how I would bear his absence, and the silence. *All splintered in my head and cried for you*, wrote Stephen Spender. I knew now what he meant. All splintered in my head and cried for Cocker.

I couldn't write poetry like Stephen Spender. But I sat down and wrote the first draft of the lines that I've ended the last chapter with. *Your eyes full of me, and your backpack full of paper books.*

I could have cried into the silence very easily that morning but I did not. I guessed that Cocker would be buttoning it and not letting a tear drop. If he did not, then neither would I.

I wanted to phone him but I didn't know what to say, or how to say it. I dreaded the possibility that we might both break down in tears. I also dreaded the possibility that we would not. That we'd manufacture a macho tone as we said, 'You all right, mate?' 'Yeah. You?' As the rest of the world does daily while, unobserved, it cries its heart out.

I texted him instead. I wrote, *You all right, mate?*

He texted back a minute later. *Yeah. You?*

I phoned Alex. I suggested we had a drink this evening. He was up for that. We agreed on The Rising Sun at Lynmouth. That was roughly halfway between our two places. Alex would borrow his mother's car. I would borrow my mother's and drive down Countisbury Hill.

Countisbury Hill, if you don't know it, is one of the scarier drives in the UK. It's carved out of the side of a cliff, it's one in five, and if you blew a tyre going down you'd be in the drink. I wasn't the bravest of drivers, but to meet Alex I'd have driven down twenty Countisbury Hills. To meet Cocker ... well, the number didn't bear thinking about. But it wasn't Cocker I was going to meet.

The Rising Sun was cosy and oak-beamed. Its frontage sort of climbed a steep seaside street. It was nice to see Alex sitting in there, waiting for me, sipping a pint. More than nice, actually. It was really lovely.

Less than three months had passed since we'd seen each other. But somehow he looked quite changed. That he was nursing a pint of bitter these days, rather than a half of lager and lime, was one of the smaller details. No doubt I looked quite altered in his eyes too. Going to university, acquiring a boyfriend – or fiend... Those things do change people a lot.

He got up when he saw me, came to the bar with me and bought me a pint. When we sat down again I said almost at once, 'So you're fixed up with a bloke? I didn't know...'

Alex cut me off. 'I didn't know either. I didn't know about you, I mean, but actually I didn't even know about myself.'

I said, 'Yeah. It's funny what going to university does.' I asked him, 'How did you meet?'

'At Freshers' Ball,' Alex said. 'I just saw this rather lost pair of eyes staring into mine. We got talking, had a few drinks, then at the end of the evening we went back to his room for coffee... and that was it.'

'Funny,' I said. 'It was Freshers' Ball started it for Cocker and me too. Though we didn't know until a few weeks later what it was the start of.' I told him how Cocker had gone to the ball but I hadn't. How I'd met Giles instead, been cuddled by him, and then got tearful when I got back to my room with Cocker, and got into his bed... 'Only we agreed the next morning not to do it again,' I said. 'That changed gradually, though, as the weeks passed.'

'Oh,' said Alex. 'There was no gradually with me and Kieran. After that first night we never looked back. Cocker, though... What a wonderful name. Does he have a wonderful cock?'

It was weird to be talking with Alex, whom I'd known for years, about other people's cocks. We'd never even talked about our own. 'I think it's wonderful,' I said. 'But it's not especially big. Only fractionally bigger than mine.' I realised that Alex wouldn't know what that meant. He'd never seen mine. I'd never seen his.

'Kieran's is huge,' Alex said, matter-of-factly. 'About twice the size of mine.' Again, I didn't know what that meant. Alex stood about five feet eleven, against my five foot seven and Cocker's five eight. You can make a rough deduction from that, but in the end it's only a guess. Alex went on, talking about Kieran's dick. 'The first time he took his trousers off, there it was poking up out of his underpants, inches of it above the waistband. He's circumcised, interestingly.'

I didn't even know if Alex was. 'And you?' I asked.

'No.' He paused. 'I don't know if you are.'

'I'm not,' I said. 'And Cocker isn't. Giles is.'

By this time I was hard inside my pants. I couldn't see, because the table was between us, whether Alex was. Though I could guess. I said, a bit diffidently, 'Do you – um – fuck each other?'

'No,' said Alex, equally diffidently. 'We haven't done that yet.'

'Nor have we,' I said, to put him at his ease. 'We just do the usual. You know.' Alex did know. He nodded. 'But the main thing is...'

'I know that too,' Alex said. 'You're both in love.' I must have given him a surprised look. He explained, 'It's in your face.'

'And in yours too, of course,' I said, suddenly realising why he looked so changed since I'd seen him last.

'Yes,' he said. 'Nice, isn't it?'

'Where does he live?' I asked.

'Exeter,' he said.

'Not *too* far,' I said. 'Cocker's in Tunbridge Wells.'

Alex pulled a face. 'That is a bit of a hike. I'm meeting up with Kieran in a couple of days. It'd be nice if you two could meet.'

I thought, how nice if Cocker could come too. Perhaps not at quite such short notice as that. But being with Alex now was giving me confidence. If he could borrow his mum's car and drive to Exeter to meet a boyfriend, surely I could ask Cocker down for a few days after Christmas. Simply tell my parents I wanted to have a friend come and stay. They'd spot it, of course, when they saw us together. Or would they? And did it matter if they did?

I texted Cocker there and then. I'd already told him I was meeting Alex this evening, but not that Alex had a boyfriend. Now I just wrote simply that I was going to meet Alex's boyfriend soon, and that I wanted Cocker to come down and stay after Christmas. He texted back with a yes to that, and we arranged a time when I could phone him when we were both private.

It was lovely to talk to Alex. We had two pints, then split. On the way out we went into the gents' together and stood side by side. After our earlier conversation we were both curious now to see the other's dick. They were hard again by the time we took them out. 'Nice cock you got,' I said, as I watched him start – with a bit of initial difficulty – to piss. It was quite a bit bigger than Cocker's, and considerably bigger than mine. If Alex thought his boyfriend's dick was enormous, then obviously it was.

Alex looked across at mine appraisingly. 'I think yours looks lovely too.'

I really wanted to grab hold of Alex's, and I could hear from the tremor in his voice that he wanted to touch mine too. We didn't dare say that we wanted to, because then we'd have done it immediately afterwards, there'd be no stopping us, and all hell would have broken loose. Alex and Kieran, Cocker and me... Things would have got messed up, to say the very least.

For obvious reasons it took quite a while for us both to empty out. But eventually we did. Then we reluctantly stowed away our cocks, which were still half stiff. Alex looked at me. 'That was difficult,' he said.

'What? Pissing or putting them away?' I said.

'Both.' Alex laughed a bit painfully. 'And for more than just one reason. You know what I mean.'

'I know,' I said.

Still we didn't move from where we stood. Alex said, 'Just a quick kiss would be all right, wouldn't it?'

'Sure,' I said. Then very quickly we kissed each other on the lips, and hugged each other briefly. It was perhaps just as well that we heard someone opening the door at that moment. That caused us to flick apart, and then out we walked, said our goodnights on the pavement without further hugs or kisses, and went to our cars.

This was the moment I'd arranged to speak to Cocker. From inside my mother's car I called him up. But the wonderful joy of hearing his voice was dimmed a little by the knowledge that I'd just kissed Alex on the lips and that I wouldn't be able to tell Cocker that. Before that moment I hadn't realised the power of something as simple as a chaste kiss.

Still, the damage wasn't that bad. It was lovely to talk. We discussed the plan for Cocker's post-Christmas visit. It was only a week away now. It didn't seem too bad. He was curious now about the fact I had a friend who had a boyfriend. He wanted to know if Alex's parents knew about that. I said they probably thought they were just good friends, and it would probably be the same with my parents and us.

Cocker had met up with some school friends earlier in the day, he said. I felt absurdly jealous for a moment. Boys or girls? I asked. Both, said Cocker. I couldn't help wondering if he'd kissed any of them and wouldn't be able to tell me about it. I was learning day by day a little more about love. Today's lesson had been about the curious effects of guilt.

I set off up Countisbury Hill. On the scary side of the road. Going up, on the left, you were just inches from the sheer drop.

Sometimes things happen in the wrong order, and before you're ready for them. My mother was lying in wait for me in the living-room when I got back. 'Thank you for driving safely and being sensible,' she said.

'Daddy and I were talking earlier. We wanted to tell you that if there was anyone special you wanted to invite down here over the holidays – I mean vacation – they'd be very welcome.'

'Oh right,' I said. 'Because there is someone I'd like to invite. I've just been on the phone to him. It's my roommate Cocker Davis.'

She tried not to let me see the fall of her face. But I did see it, and it told me a terrible lot. Then she brightened quickly. 'We'd thought you might want to ask a girl down. But if it's your friend Cocker, well, that's fine with us.'

I felt myself getting frightened and not knowing what to do. I wanted Cocker. He'd know what to say. I had to do my best. 'Maybe I'll bring a girl next time,' I flannelled. 'In the meantime, though, I'll ask Cocker, if that's OK with you. He's like Alex. Just a mate.'

I couldn't look my mother in the eye at that moment. I'd lied to her about the biggest and best thing in my life. I'd shafted Cocker behind his back. I'd been a coward. Did I feel a total shit? Yes I did.

Alex drove us down to Exeter. Skirting Exmoor. We met Kieran at The Ship. Kieran was kind of my size, and of course the first thing I thought about was the fact that, unlike me, he had an amazingly big cock. The second was that he had a lovely face, and the third was that when he spoke to me he was absolutely charming. By the time we'd all had a drink and a sandwich I had realised that if I'd met Kieran instead of Cocker during Freshers' Week we'd have fallen for each other. That was this day's lesson about love.

Afterwards the three of us wandered around the streets for a bit. I could sense the frustration of the other two. After a bit I said, 'Look, if you two want to go off somewhere together, just do it. We'll meet up later.'

Alex said, 'Yes, but where?'

Public toilets? I wondered, but that didn't seem very nice. I didn't suggest it. 'Use the car,' I said.

'My mum's car?' Alex said. I could hear in his voice that he had difficulties with that.

'Needs must,' I said, to strengthen him. 'Just go for it.' I walked with them back to the multi-storey where we'd put it and we went up in the lift. 'I'll stand guard,' I said when we got to the right floor. 'But at a discreet distance. I promise not to look.'

I took up a position midway between the lift and the car and politely turned my back. But it turned out that not looking was at least as thought-provoking as looking would have been. I soon found my hand in my pocket, stroking my cock through the lining. I forced myself to stop. To take my mind off it I texted Cocker and told him what I was doing. *You got some crazy friends,* he texted back. It didn't seem he was upset at least.

A few minutes later Alex and Kieran and I were back in town, looking for somewhere to get a cup of tea. I told them I'd had to text Cocker to stop myself wanking. Both Alex and Kieran had wicked smiles on their faces that they couldn't shift even for politeness's sake. 'I'd like to meet Cocker,' Kieran said. 'He sounds great.'

'He is,' I said.

THIRTEEN

I met Alex and Kieran again a couple of days later. Kieran came up to Porlock Weir and we had a walk along the beach. 'Do your parents know?' I asked both of them. 'Have they sussed the two of you yet?'

They looked at each other. 'Don't think so,' they both said, though there was a bit of doubt in both their voices.

I said, 'I think mine are onto Cocker and me. They're still talking about wanting me to get a girlfriend.'

'That's the trouble with being an only child,' Kieran said. 'It's easier for me. My elder brother and his girlfriend are in the spotlight. I can hide in the shadows a bit.'

'Same here,' said Alex. 'My sister and her boyfriend. My sexuality is still a bit invisible at the moment, like Kieran's.'

I said, faux-naively and a bit unkindly perhaps, 'Do you think that will last for ever?'

Alex sighed and said, 'No, obviously not. Buying time is all I'm doing, I guess.' While Kieran appeared to be biting his lip.

Christmas Day was almost upon us. It's a day when even declared lovers are often parted by the expectations of their parents, while those who haven't yet declared themselves stand no chance. We talked about this as we walked among the rocks, while little flocks of oystercatchers rose up from near our feet from time to time and flew piping tunefully ahead of us. Christmas was going to be a day, we all agreed, when we'd have to be careful about contacting each other too often or too blatantly if we wanted to avoid letting our parents guess too much. We and the absent Cocker would simply have to put things on hold for twenty-four hours. At least we'd all be meeting up again – the four of us with any luck – a couple of days after that.

OK. Don't knock Christmas, I told myself. It's a family time. There's warmth and a feeling of celebration, and plenty to eat and drink. And at my place there were more than just the three of us. My mother's sister and her two kids came round for dinner in the afternoon. And my mother was a good cook. We were just finishing the pudding when the house phone rang. 'Whoever phones up at this time on Christmas Day?' my mother asked rhetorically as she got up to answer it. The Queen had only just finished her TV broadcast.

She came back into the room with a rather inscrutable look on her face. 'It's for you,' she said to me. 'Your friend Cocker.'

My young cousins, one a boy of fourteen and the other a girl of twelve, collapsed in hysterics. 'Whoever has a name like Cocker?!' the fourteen-year-old managed to get out. I got up and went out into the hall.

'Cocker,' I said as I picked the handset up. 'Happy Christmas, mate.'

'Happy...' he began, but then his voice collapsed onto a sob. 'Oh fuck,' he said, in a voice that wouldn't hold up.

'Cocker, what's wrong?' I said, and felt everything mound up inside me all at once. I knew what it was.

'I fucking miss you. I can't bear it...' And I heard my big strong Cocker, my big tough little Cocker weeping at the other end of a phone line, from two hundred miles' distance.

I just started crying too. I think it was from shock as much as anything else. But I had to get myself under control quickly. If anyone heard me and came out into the hall... 'Cocker, where are you?' I asked.

'Sitting on the stairs,' he said. The words came out between heaves of his breath. 'The others are eating nuts. I said I wanted a breath of fresh air...' But evidently the stairs was as far as he'd got.

'We're going to be together in two days, darling,' I said to him desperately, then realised what I'd just said. I looked around in panic. The door from the hall into the dining-room was a few inches open. Laughter came from the other side of it. But had anyone heard what I'd called Cocker? 'I can't talk properly here,' I said. 'I'm in the hall, and someone'll come out. 'Call me on my own phone when we're both in bed tonight. Say...' Oh lord, what time do other people's families go to bed on Christmas Day? 'Say quarter past midnight, if that's not too late.'

Cocker managed to say that would be about right. Then he said, 'I love you, Pip. Talk later.' And rang off.

'Is your friend all right?' my mother asked innocently enough as I re-entered the room. 'I thought he sounded a bit upset.'

'Oh, he's OK,' I said brightly. 'Just wanted to say Happy Christmas.'

Then the twelve-year-old (out of the mouths of babes and sucklings) said, 'You look like you've been crying, Pip.'

'No, I haven't!' I lied cheerfully. 'Why ever would I do that?' I risked discovering that she knew the answer to that dangerous, bluffing question and would publicly announce it. But thank heaven, she did not.

I was in bed, naked under the duvet a few minutes after twelve o'clock. I was quite sleepy, as I'd had a bit to drink. I held my phone in one hand. My other hand... Well, I don't need to tell you where that was.

It flashed – I'd set it to silent mode – a few minutes later. I mean my phone flashed. Not my cock.

We spoke in whispers under the bedclothes. The bedclothes of two beds that were two hundred miles apart. 'I'm sorry I upset you this afternoon,' he said.

'I'm sorry you were upset,' I told him. We were quite calm and dignified now. Almost businesslike. 'It's a bummer, Christmas. I mean for people like us.'

'Too right,' he said.

'You in bed?' I asked him.

'Yeah.'

'You naked or in jim-jams?'

'Bollock-naked,' he said matter-of-factly. ''Cept for the duvet, of course. You?'

'Ditto,' I answered. 'How's your cock?'

'Just giving it a feel as you asked the question,' he said. 'It's about half-mast. And yours?'

I felt it carefully. 'Standing about ten to tummy,' I said.

He said, 'Fancy a Christmas wank?'

I said, 'Technically it's now Boxing Day.'

'Don't split pubic hairs,' he said.

We went for it anyway, each to our own in our separate beds, keeping the phone line open and talking our way through it. When we'd both finished we agreed it was one of the best Christmas presents we could have given each other. In those circumstances, at any rate.

'How the hell did people manage before telephones?' Cocker asked.

I had no answer to that.

Two days later Cocker arrived in person. I met him at Exeter St David's. I was pretty anonymous in Exeter, almost as anonymous as he was, so we risked a hug and a quick kiss inside the station. Actually, we didn't weigh the risk up, we just did it. We needed it so much.

I drove Cocker home over Exmoor. Along the wild high road through Dulverton and Simonsbath. I showed

Exmoor off to Cocker as if I owned it all. We stopped along the way, of course. In an opening that led to a field gate. We'd already had our hands all over each other as we drove along. Once we'd stopped we simply pulled our jeans down a little way and tugged each other off. It only took a couple of seconds: we needed each other so much. But we were careful to keep our thighs pressed together as we came all over them. I didn't want stuff spilling over my mum's car seats.

I took him home. It hadn't been home, my parents' house, during the past week or two. It had lacked a Cocker. Now it had one. It was home once more. Home was where Cocker was.

By the time we got back, of course, this being late December, it was nearly dark. I wanted to show Cocker everything at once, but couldn't do it tonight. We had an earlyish supper, then went out. We were going to meet Alex in the pub at Lynmouth, The Rising Sun. I was looking forward to that. It meant driving down precipitous Countisbury Hill, down the face of the granite cliff. I did it nonchalantly. I showed off my driving skills and my nerves of steel to Cocker. I wasn't scared in the slightest. So much depends on who you're with.

I was learning, not from what he said, but from what he did, that our ten days' separation had hurt Cocker even more dreadfully than it had hurt me. He couldn't take his hands off me, except in the presence of my parents, and even that, I could see, was difficult. On the drive down Countisbury Hill his hands were inside my fly, which he'd unzipped. Maybe some of my new confidence on that scary slope was to do with that.

He liked Alex at once. I was relieved by that. I was even more relieved by the fact that he didn't like him inconveniently too much. And Alex liked Cocker too, of course.

'Do you share a room with Kieran?' was one of the first things Cocker thought to ask my old friend.

'No such luck,' said Alex, while Cocker started to rub his hand up the top of my thigh under the table – it was something he'd never done in Oxford in such a public place. 'But we're in the same hall. It's a trip along a few corridors. We do alternate venues alternate nights. We get seen sometimes, but I don't think anyone's actually twigged.'

'They will,' said Cocker. 'You need to be ready for that.' He turned to me. 'Have you told him about the reception we got in hall that night, and our names on the door being reversed?'

'I told him about the dinner thing,' I said. 'Not about the door.' So Cocker proceeded to do that.

Alex guffawed. 'All the years I've known you, Mr Rogers, and I'd never thought of that. Took your surname for granted. Pip rogers Cocker Davis. I like that.' Then he stopped and gave me an uncomfortable look. He was obviously remembering our conversation of a few days earlier. The one in which we'd both admitted that we and our respective partners didn't actually fuck.

Wc had two pints each. We drank them slowly because we were all enjoying one another's company so much. But there was no way I was going to drink more than that. I had the climb back up Countisbury Hill to face. We arranged to meet again next day at Porlock, with Kieran this time. Before we all left we trooped into the gents' together. We made no secret of looking at one another's dicks while we emptied our bladders, and all three of them were half stiff. But none of us commented, and no-one risked a kiss. Instead we all hugged one another politely on the pavement as we parted for the night.

Cocker had his arm around my shoulder, and was rubbing my crotch with the other one as we ascended the hill on dipped headlights. We made it to the top. I always did in the end, but it always seemed a bit of an event. The best bit of the day still lay ahead of us, though. There were two spare bedrooms in our house, either of which Cocker could have slept in. But there were two single beds in my room. Without discussing it my mother had made the innocent assumption that we'd want to share a room together, and had made up the second bed in my room for my friend.

To avoid shocking her we made sure that both beds were slept in eventually, though only mine was occupied all night. Even before we got into it together our hands were exploring each other inch by inch, like dogs re-marking their territories after they've been away from them for a bit. And then... well, I won't bore you with it. We did what we always did. Only it seemed more wonderful than ever.

Afterwards Cocker said, 'On the phone on Christmas Day, when I was losing it, you called me darling. It seemed a bit odd, two blokes, you know, but … actually I wouldn't mind if you went on doing it.'

'Only if you say it to me first,' I said.

'Darling Pip.' He whispered it. It made the hairs on the back of my neck rise and my arms tingled. I hadn't known that would happen. Hadn't known the power of it. 'First time I've used the word to anyone,' he said, still in a whisper.

'Darling Cocker,' I said. I tried for a normal voice. But mine too came out as a whisper. I hadn't expected that either. I tried another phrase I'd never used before in its entirety. It too was a whisper, of course. 'My darling, I love you so much.'

He said, 'I love you *all* much.'

We actually walked all the way to Porlock Weir in the morning. It's about five miles, but the sea views from the cliff path are so spectacular that you don't notice the distance. And there was nobody else about on that gorse-flanked track, or hardly anybody, so as we walked we could throw our arms around each other's shoulders from time to time. And we did.

'Middle of winter and there's still a few yellow flowers about,' Cocker said, looking at the sea of scrub around us.

'It's gorse,' I said.

'I thought it was,' he said, blustering a little. As a doctor's son he knew he was expected to know about things like that.

But I knew he wouldn't know about the next bit. 'When the gorse is not in bloom, then kissing's out of season. Old country saying.'

'I like it,' said Cocker, and turned and gave me a smacker on the lips.

It's quite funny explaining to people that you live in a village made famous by a classic novel, when you've never made it all the way through the novel yourself and the person you're explaining to hasn't even attempted it. We lived in the remote hamlet of Oare, where Exmoor tips down vertiginously towards the cliffs of the Bristol Channel. 'Oare was where John Ridd came from,' I told Cocker. We'd had better things to do and say last night than for me to go into this.

'John Ridd?'

'Hero of Lorna Doone. Some of the book was written in the pub we went to last night.' We were dropping down into the fold of the cliff that hides Culbone church. Atmospheric and in the middle of nowhere, this tiny chapel beside the sea was where John and Lorna married.

'I guess the book was a romance,' Cocker said.

'I suppose it was,' I said. 'But there are six hundred pages of it. Plus.'

Cocker looked me very steadily in the eye. 'I hope there'll be six hundred pages of us.'

Fucking hell. How this guy broke me up...

FOURTEEN

We met at The Ship, right by the sea at Porlock Weir. It was a cosy, thatched inn about five hundred years old, with low ceilings and mullioned windows. I enjoyed showing it off now to Cocker. Alex and Kieran arrived about a minute after us. They'd driven back from Exeter where, wonder of wonders, Alex had stayed the night with Kieran at his parents' house.

'You still sure they suspect nothing?' Cocker asked, after he and Kieran had been introduced.

Alex and Kieran looked at each other. 'Too soon to say,' said Kieran and shrugged.

Cocker took to Kieran instantly, as I knew he would. Cocker, Alex and I were all quite good-looking in a regular sort of way. But Kieran outclassed the three of us in that department. He had film-star looks, and the charm to go with them. And yet I was able to put aside a doubt I'd had when I'd first met him. Had I met both him and Cocker at the same time during Freshers' Week, Cocker would still have been the one I'd have fallen for. Now they were both in the same room with me I no longer had any uncertainty about that. Even if – though I only had Alex's word for this – Kieran did have a massive dick.

We worked our lunch off with a bracing walk on Porlock beach. Later Alex drove us back to Oare on his way to his parents'. In the evening we all met up again in The Rising Sun... By now I was driving up and down that treacherous hill with complete insouciance.

The next couple of days passed in similar fashion. There were walks on Exmoor, drives out to country pubs, and nights that I spent in tight embrace with Cocker, and Kieran with Alex. We were all in heaven, of course. But then, all too soon, it was time for Cocker to depart. There was a family thing over the New Year that his parents wanted him to be at, and like a good boy – and so as not to draw too much attention to his need for my company – he'd said yes.

'It's not too long till the beginning of term,' I consoled him on the platform of Exeter St David's. 'Less than a fortnight.'

'It still seems too long,' he said. 'Being without you hurts.'

Less than six months ago we'd been schoolboys still. If anyone had told us we'd so soon be longing for the start of an academic term we'd have laughed in disbelief.

'We'll phone. We'll text,' I tried to comfort him. 'We can do long-distance wanks.'

'It's not the same,' he said. 'When I'm without you everything in my head breaks in pieces. I just want to run away from everything and be with you.' That was roughly what Stephen Spender had written. It shook me to hear Cocker come out with it. 'I didn't know it was going to be like this.'

We were both learning love's lessons. 'You're making me cry,' I said.

He threw himself around me as we stood among the post-Christmas crowds awaiting trains. I felt the whole of his body shaking. He seemed to be trying to burrow inside me, as a mole burrows into earth. I was trying to do the same to him. We were both in tears by now, of course.

We no longer cared what kind of exhibition we were making of ourselves. Our feelings were too big and too important for us to bother about that. Nobody we knew would see us anyway... But I was wrong about that. As Cocker's London-bound train drew in I saw that one of the other people boarding it further down the platform was my father's partner in his veterinary practice. He gave me a curt wave as Cocker and I reluctantly disentangled ourselves. He must have seen, even if he hadn't watched us intently, the emotional nature of our embrace.

I didn't mention this to Cocker then. He had enough other stuff to deal with. 'Love you, Cockerfuckercocker,' I said, as the doors between us began to flash and bleep. And because it was one syllable shorter he just had time to say, 'Love you, Cockerfuckerpip,' as they swished shut.

One hour gone. Only another 287 to wait. That was the opening of his first text to me from the train. I hadn't quite got back to Oare yet. I stopped the car and texted back. *We can both get a train an hour earlier. Then it's only 286.* We texted and phoned jokily throughout the rest of that day. I couldn't believe how the emptiness of this second parting in the space of a fortnight would hurt. I couldn't believe how reasonable I'd been about things on the station platform. The experience of separating from him at the end of term should have taught me what to expect. Cocker had felt it first, but now it was me. I hadn't known how I'd look my mother in the eye when I got back to the house. In the end I'd got through it somehow – I was an actor after all, wasn't I? – but only just.

Kieran and Alex were lovely and supportive during those 286 hours. I spent quite a lot of time with them. But not too much. I didn't want to be a gooseberry. Nor did I want to take too much advantage of something I had – contact with other gay friends – that Cocker, back in Tunbridge Wells, did not. If he was suffering, I wanted to suffer with him. Any of you psychologists? Make what you will of that.

Three days before the start of term – we were down to about 76 hours, give or take – a letter arrived from the college. I opened it, a bit unsure what to expect. The letter told me there had been a reallocation of college rooms. My new address would be room 8 on staircase 6 of the King George wing. The letter was signed by the college bursar.

I held the paper in my hand for some moments, like a South Sea Islander confronting a bottle with a written message in it. I was just as perplexed by the meaning of what I was looking at. I called Cocker, and he was there at once. 'Have you had a letter?' I asked.

'Room reallocation? Yep.'

I butted in. 'King George wing. Staircase six, room eight.'

'Lawson Building,' Cocker said. His voice was choked with anger. 'Room twenty-six.'

'Why the fuck...?' I said. I felt a pit opening up. We spoke together, interrupting and cutting in on each other's thoughts. 'We'll challenge it...' 'Write them a letter...' 'Take it up with...' 'Now or when we get there?' I don't know which one of us said what bits of that. Perhaps both of us said all of it.

We did nothing of course. In the end they were the college and we were just two kids.

The hours were counting down. By the time my mother drove me to Exeter for the train to London – in that car of hers that had seen so much recent action she knew nothing about – they'd got down to three point six.

I got out of the car and kissed her, as I was getting my luggage out of the boot. 'It's been a good holiday – I mean vacation,' I said.

'Yes,' Mum said. 'It was lovely to meet Cocker.' She paused. 'Just give me a second of your time,' she said. She looked down for a moment, then looked back into my face. 'I know what's happening between you,' she said. 'I know how lovely it is at the moment, and I don't want to say anything against that.'

'Mum...' I protested, but it cut no ice.

'What you don't know,' she went on, 'is that life can get even better than that. When you find a girlfriend one day you'll understand what I've just said. It's something you're going through, I know...'

'Mum, can you just stop it. I'm in love with Cocker. He's in love with me. Nothing will ever be better than that for either of us...' It looks calm written down, but it was anything but. My voice was climbing a steep gradient. My feelings too. She tried to catch me by the elbows but I twisted out of her grasp. I burst into tears and ran away from her, crying. I shoved my ticket into the slot in the barrier. I heard her distraught cry behind me. 'Pip! My darling Pip!'

I'd just discovered what hell was like. I didn't look back.

Cocker's face came out of a crowd and into focus as we met at Paddington station under the clock.

If I ever do get back,
Will you still be there?
Motionless,
At the top of the subway?
With your eyes full of me,
And your backpack
Full of paper books?

The miracle had happened. The miracle we call the passage of time. I had got back. And Cocker was there, waiting for me. With his eyes full of me. Never mind the backpack and the paper books.

We talked on the train. A lot of it was painful stuff. But we were together again. There was no pain that could overcome that.

We wheeled our luggage rattlingly up Hythebridge Street and signed in at the porter's lodge. 'We'd better take our stuff up to our rooms and meet up in twenty,' I said. 'Tea at your place?'

'Tea at my place in twenty for sure,' Cocker said. 'But we're not spending twenty minutes apart just yet. I'm coming up with you to yours. When you're settled we come down and get me into my place. Understood?'

Cocker dragged his own baggage all the way, up three floors, to my room. He actually opened his suitcase and took out a shirt. 'Wear this for me tomorrow,' he said.

I hadn't thought of that. I unpacked one of mine and gave it to him. 'Wear this for me tomorrow,' I said.

My Georgian room, high ceilinged and with two big sash windows, would have been lovely had I been sharing it with Cocker. But I wouldn't be sharing it with Cocker. So it was hateful to me. Every cubic inch of it.

I was astonished then to hear Cocker say, as if he'd read my thought, 'You'll like the room when I've shared your bed in it. Tonight. Unless we decide to christen mine first.'

The rest of that evening was an irrelevant prelude to bedtime, although it was nice enough. Tea with Cocker in the Lawson Building. Dinner in hall with other friends, and catching up. Drinks with mates afterwards at the Lamb and Flag. People were quite shocked by the news that Cocker and I had been split up. We'd been kind of outed by the dinner-time incident at the end of last term, and people had had the whole of the Christmas vac to digest the fact that we were a couple. So far no-one seemed to find anything wrong with that. 'Challenge it,' they all said.

'In the morning,' we said.

We spent the night together in my bed. As Cocker had predicted so wisely, by the time morning came the room seemed quite nice.

We went together to the bursar's office. His assistant told us he was busy, but he heard our voices at the door and came out to talk to us. 'Is it about the room change?' he asked. His tone was perfectly friendly. We said yes, it was. 'There's nothing I can do to alter that,' he said. 'The decision came from the master. If you want to discuss it, well, you'll have to take it up with him. You'll need to make an appointment.'

Our faces must have fallen, as he smiled at us rather nicely and said, 'Would you like me to save you one hurdle at least, and make an appointment with him now?' We said yes, a bit timidly, and he immediately went back to his desk and called the master – or his secretary – up. He looked up at us a few seconds and a few sentences later. 'What about six o'clock this evening?' he asked. 'How would that suit?' We said we were fine with that.

As we were walking away from his office I got a text. It was from James. (The man I'd once called Ponytail: he'd directed us in Hamlet.) He had a project he wanted to discuss with Cocker and me. Could we meet after college dinner? Half past eight in The Randolph? I checked with Cocker, then texted back. We'd be there, I said. The Morse bar was expensive. I hoped James would be paying for the drinks – though I didn't put that in my text.

We had never met the master, let alone been to his house. We saw him at dinner in hall quite often, especially when it was a formal one at which we all had to wear our gowns, but that was about it. Third year students were invited to the master's house for ritual cocktails, but for Cocker and me that was still two years ahead. All the colleges at Oxford had rather splendid 'master's lodgings', but ours was one of the best. It formed an attachment to the end of the King George wing, and was in itself a perfectly formed Georgian house, overlooking the college gardens and the lake. We rang the bell with a certain amount of trepidation. As we waited for it to be answered I said to Cocker, 'I think I'd rather be driving down Countisbury Hill.'

'At least there was a pub at the bottom of it,' Cocker said.

The master, a bald, bespectacled man who had once been a Prime Minister's private secretary, came to the door himself. He showed us into his tapestried sitting-room. The tapestries were magnificent. They depicted forest scenes, with maidens and unicorns and fierce-toothed lions roaming about among the tress. Between them the enormous floor-length curtains were drawn shut. Had it been daylight outside we'd have had a view of the college gardens and the lake.

'Sit down,' the master said, indicating a sofa to us both. He wasn't stuffy or pompous. 'The sun's over the yard-arm. Can I suggest a dry sherry, gentlemen?'

We were too surprised to say no, and watched as he poured us a glass each from a bottle of Tio Pepe that stood on the sideboard, and one for himself. But then he became more serious as he installed himself in an arm-chair opposite us. 'I think you've come to talk about your room allocation,' he said. 'Is that correct?'

'Yes,' I said, and Cocker nodded his head.

'Do I take it you're not happy with the new arrangement?'

'That's right,' Cocker said. 'We liked sharing a room together and now you've parted us.'

The master sighed almost imperceptibly. 'I'm sorry that's the way you feel, but you really haven't given me much choice.'

'How's that?' I asked.

'I'm afraid you're rather high-profile, the pair of you. Two young men who share a room together might sleep together occasionally and nobody be any the wiser. But that's not exactly your case, is it?' We said nothing. He went on. 'Your relationship was actually hinted at in the press. And it was very publicly aired that night at dinner last term.'

'But we weren't responsible for either of those things,' I protested. 'We'd have been perfectly happy to keep our heads down, and our relationship under wraps. It wasn't our fault that other people made a big thing about it.'

'But people did,' the master said. 'The result was that the entire college, and probably other people around the university, became aware that a couple were sharing a room together. Well, the college doesn't put people into shared accommodation on the basis of their personal relationships. And let me make it clear that there's no distinction made here between relationships between people of the same, and people of the opposite, sex. If I let this stand as a precedent, half the college would be asking to move into rooms they could share with their girl- or boyfriends. They'd say quite reasonably that if you could do it, so could they.'

'But if a pair of students came up who were already married...' Cocker said.

'Then we would normally help them to find a flat, or rooms in somebody's house.' The master gave Cocker a piercing look. 'If you felt that strongly about the situation, you yourselves could consider those options.'

I wasn't sure what I thought about that. I'd need to discuss it with Cocker...

At that moment I was astonished to hear Cocker come out with, 'Supposing we went and got a civil partnership?'

The master also looked startled for a moment. Then he recovered himself. 'That wouldn't necessarily assure you of a shared room in college. But more seriously, a civil partnership is a rather major commitment, just as marriage is. People do get married in order to try and get a council house, I realise, but it's not the best of motives, and happy marriages do not always result. You two are only just eighteen. That might be a bit young for a civil partnership, don't you think? Especially if it was just for the sake of a double room for a few months.' He paused and sipped his sherry. Then he stood up. 'Gentlemen, I'm sorry, but my decision stands. If you do decide at some stage that you'd like to move out of college and into some other kind of accommodation, please feel free to come back and talk about that.' He shook our hands and showed us out into the dark.

FIFTEEN

The thousand natural shocks that flesh is heir to, I'd said in character as Hamlet night after night. I seemed to be receiving quite a few of those shocks right now, I thought, as I walked back from the master's house with Cocker. There had been the bursar's letter, then the dreadful scene with my mother at the station, and now here was Cocker springing the idea of a civil partnership. Six weeks ago he hadn't seen the two of us as even being in a gay relationship. I wouldn't know until I asked him whether he was just making a point or if he was actually serious about that.

'So, what do we do?' Cocker broke the silence.

I said, 'Maybe go to the college bar for a swift half before dinner?'

'Best idea yet,' Cocker said.

We drank those half pints in a rather pregnant near-silence, only occasionally talking about what the master had said, and then only in the most general terms. Neither of us was ready to bring up the civil partnership business yet. We were both frightened by the sudden seriousness of everything, I think.

After dinner we made our way to The Randolph. James was already there, ensconced in one of the armchairs, beneath the glittering chandeliers and the white ceiling vault. Perhaps deliberately he'd chosen the seat that was the favourite of Colin Dexter, the creator of Morse. Though James was no longer Mr Ponytail. He'd shaved his head. It looked like an egg. I thought he looked frightful but I didn't tell him that.

We sat down in two more armchairs and to my relief James ordered our drinks. Then he outlined his proposal. He wanted to direct a production of R. C. Sherriff's classic, Journey's End, this term. But he only wanted to do it if I would play one of the two leading characters, Raleigh, and Cocker play the other one, Stanhope.

I was thrilled. Doesn't seem too cool to be saying that, but it was true. I knew the play, and loved it. We'd read it at school. Cocker hadn't heard of it. I told him about it. 'It's a beautiful play. Set in the trenches of the First World War. The friendship between Raleigh and Stanhope is wonderful. It's not sentimental but very, very moving. They're both very young, Raleigh just out of school. Stanhope was at the same school and knew Raleigh there. Raleigh dies at the end, more or less in Stanhope's arms, like in Hamlet. Please say you'll do it.'

'I've never thought of myself as an actor...' Cocker was hesitating, but I knew he would say yes in a moment.

'Just say yes, Cocker,' I said.

'Yes, then,' he said, and a broad triumphant grin spread over his face. Our drinks arrived at that moment.

'That's great,' said James. 'I can order the scripts and get a cast together. I thought of asking Will to do Osbourne – Uncle as the younger guys call him.' He turned to me. 'What do you think?'

I felt wonderful. James had not only offered lead roles to Cocker and me without asking us to audition, but was now even asking for my opinion about casting. I said, 'I think Will would be great.'

We stayed chatting after that while our drinks lasted, and while we were still there in walked Giles. He was with Mick, the young guy we'd met with him at the club after the Hamlet first night. They joined us. After a bit more general chat James left.

I hadn't seen Giles since before Will told me that he and Giles had fucked each other. I didn't know whether that had been just once or more often than that. Now I found myself wondering about Giles and the rather pretty Mick.

Giles might have been wondering the same thing about Cocker and me. He didn't ask, of course, but he was very keen to hear all our news. We had rather a lot of it, and now it all came pouring out. That my best mate at home had discovered he was gay and had a boyfriend whom we'd met. That I'd fallen out with my mother just yesterday and we hadn't spoken since. That we'd been moved into separate rooms. That we'd just had a disappointing chat with the master of our college about that. And then, because I felt I was in safe company, 'Cocker suggested we get a civil partnership.'

Giles and Mick rocked slightly backwards in their seats. Even Cocker seemed a bit taken aback.

'I think,' said Giles after a short pause, 'that might be rather a heavy response to the situation. Taking a sledge-hammer to crack a nut.' It was more or less what the master had said.

'You're very young,' said Mick gently. 'You don't know who you're going to meet.'

'But I know who I have met,' I said, while Cocker looked at me and said approvingly,

'You took the words out of my mouth.'

'Then I hope you'll be together for years and years,' said Giles. 'You're a perfect pair. But maybe wait a couple of years before doing the civil bit.' He and Mick looked at each other. Giles turned back to Cocker and me. 'Even we haven't thought about it yet.'

Mick said, 'It's not as though either of you's going to die any time soon. And you probably wouldn't be leaving huge investment portfolios if you did. Though correct me if I'm wrong about the last bit.'

We didn't correct him. He was right about that bit.

'I might be able to come up with a few other thoughts about that,' Mick said. 'Give me a day or two.'

'What sort of thoughts?' Cocker asked.

'Aha,' Mick said. I couldn't help seeing, from where I sat, that he had a nice little mound in his crotch. Small but prominent.

Giles said, 'Why don't the two of you come round for a drink at my place tomorrow night and we can talk about it?'

I looked at Cocker and he nodded. He said to Giles, 'That would be nice.'

'There's something you need to do before that, though, Pip,' Giles said.

'What's that?' I asked. I thought he might say something like, go home and wank Cocker off. I half hoped he would.

He said, quite seriously, 'Phone your mother. Just tell her you love her, then end the call. That's all that's needed. At least for now.' Then a mischievous look appeared on his face. 'And then go home and wank Cocker off.'

We headed back to college, to Cocker's room in the Lawson Building, after leaving The Randolph. On the way down Beaumont Street I screwed my courage up and called my mum... I did exactly what Giles had told me too. I said, 'I just called to say I love you, mum, and everything's OK. And Cocker sends his love. We'll talk soon.' Then, without waiting for her to answer, I ended the call. If she wanted to say anything mega right then she'd call me back. She did not.

It was barely ten o'clock when we got to Cocker's room but we stripped each other naked immediately. As our jeans slid down our thighs our cocks popped up already stiff. We climbed, with our appendages wagging like puppies' tails in front of us, straight into bed. Then I carried out the second part of Giles's instruction and Cocker, without needing to be told to, returned the compliment.

*

The following evening I took Cocker round to Giles's house. I knocked at the door. Mick let us in. While Cocker and I were still wearing coats and scarves this January night, as well as everything we had on underneath, Mick and Giles were clad in very indoor fashion. Each wore a lightweight jumper with nothing underneath, and cotton slacks (Giles's beige, Mick's white) with – I'd have sworn – nothing underneath those either. Giles had been similarly lacking in the underwear department the last time I'd come here, while as for Mick, when he sat down on the sofa opposite us, I could see the modest little curl of his flaccid cock (it was no bigger than mine was) through the fabric of the top of his right trouser leg. Mick was about four years older than me, I guessed. I thought he – and his cock – looked sweet.

'Jack Daniels OK for you both?' Giles asked us. We both said yes. The first time I'd been here I hadn't known what Jack Daniels was. Now, with a whole term of student life under our belts, both Cocker and I knew everything there was to know about drink.

'We've been putting our heads together,' Giles said, 'on the subject of your double room difficulty. 'We were thinking that an article in one of the local newspapers might not go amiss.'

'But who would write it?' Cocker asked. 'And who would print it if someone did?'

'Did we not tell you Mick's a journalist?' Giles said.

'No,' I said. 'I had no idea.'

Giles said, 'He wrote the review of Hamlet that you liked so much.'

Another Pip, the one in Great Expectations, writes, *the roof of my stronghold dropped upon me,* when he discovers that the person who has given him his fortune is not the genteel if daft as a brush Miss Havisham but the convict Magwitch. Well, I now felt almost like that. I'd taken the article as a wonderful compliment from a stranger. Now I knew it had been written by someone who had met me and Cocker in a gay club immediately after seeing the opening night, had seen us interacting together off-stage, and presumably fancied both of us.

It would have been overstating things to say the roof of my stronghold had dropped upon me, but I had certainly received a shock. I wasn't quite sure how I felt about it. I felt the circumstances, newly brought to our attention, in which Cocker and I had won our accolades cheapened those somewhat. But then I found myself wondering whether, behind the scenes of the world of reviews and critiques, it was often like that. I was still growing up rapidly. Though this wasn't a lesson about love, exactly, it was a lesson about life.

'But the review was written by someone called Mark Daniels,' Cocker said.

'That's a name I write under,' said Mick. 'I write under two or three different names. It depends what I'm writing about. Different fields of knowledge, different areas of interest. Nobody can be an expert on more than one subject. Or so the readers of newspapers think. So it helps to have more than one name at your disposal.' He grinned a bit bashfully at Cocker and me, and I saw his dick twitch in his trousers like a mouse.

'It's just a question of finding an angle you'd be happy with,' Giles said. 'Victimisation of gay men? One rule for straight couples, another one for us? Forced into a civil partnership by an outdated code of morality? College regulations not caught up with the modern world? What do you think?'

'Well, all of those in a way,' I said, 'but in a way none of them. What the master said was actually very reasonable; it just wasn't favourable to us. It was that rooms couldn't be allocated to people on the basis of who they fell in love with, whatever their sex. People would be swapping around endlessly if their relationships were of the short-term sort.'

'But you didn't ask for a room together,' said Mick. 'You were given a room together. It was after that, not before, that you fell in love. And because of that they're punishing you by separating you. That's how you should look at it. Let the college authorities look at the big picture. You need to fight your own corner, look at your own particular case. Like in a court of law. The master can tell his story, you tell yours. The readers of the paper then make their mind up. They're judge and jury here, not you.'

'Think it over, anyway,' Giles said. 'You don't have to decide this instant.'

'Well,' I said to Mick, a bit torn now, 'if you did want to go ahead with it, you couldn't say that all those angle things came from us.'

'I wouldn't,' said Mick. 'I promise. The story would be my own. I'd run it past you before sending it in, ask you to give me a couple of quotes, and an editor from the newspaper would phone the master to give him a chance to comment before the thing went to press. Would that be all right?'

Cocker and I looked at each other, gauging our reactions from each other's face. Slowly we began to nod. 'We think that would be all right,' Cocker said slowly, and with the gravity that befitted a statement made not just by one but by the two of us.

Then Mick looked at me and said, 'Come over here and talk to me. I haven't really got to know you yet.'

Giles said, 'In which case can I go and talk to Cocker? I haven't really got to know him yet.'

So I got up and Giles got up and we each slid into the vacant space next to each other's partner that the other had just left.

Mick and I questioned each other about all the usual things. Where we came from, career plans, areas of common interest... And as we talked I felt Mick's arm come around my shoulder, as lightly and unthreateningly as a scarf. I looked across to where Cocker was in earnest conversation with Giles and saw that Giles's arm was also laid carelessly along the back of his sofa, just brushing the back of Cocker's neck.

Cocker seemed all right with Giles's arm there. In which case, I was all right with Mick's.

'But you still manage to sleep together,' Mick was saying to me. 'That's all OK, isn't it?'

'It's OK,' I said. 'We went to my room the first night of term, to Cocker's last night... We plan to alternate. It does mean one of us has to get up early, though, before the scouts start work at half past eight. We haven't risked a lie-in yet, and being caught.'

'But other students must know, surely,' Mick said.

'Oh yes,' I said. 'They're all fine with it. I told him how we'd been 'outed' at dinner at the end of the last term. And remembering, added, 'And that was all because of your review of Hamlet, come to think of it.'

'Oh dear,' said Mick, and gave my shoulder a tweak. 'So it's my fault in the end that you lost your room together. Then it's more than ever my intention to write something that puts it right.'

Giles had left Cocker's side for a moment, just long enough to top up everyone's Jack Daniels. Then he returned to his chat with my mate. Mick said, quite close to my ear now, 'Does Cocker know about you and Giles last term?'

I said, 'Yes, I made a clean breast of it. He was a bit funny about it at first, but then accepted it. After all, it happened before he and I got serious.' I paused, then said, 'Actually I wasn't sure you knew about it.'

'Well, these things happen,' Mick said. 'Giles and I have a fairly open relationship, I suppose you'd say. We're not together all of the time. We usually tell each other about things that have happened.' He paused. 'Although sometimes not till quite a long time afterwards.'

I said, 'I don't think Cocker and I are planning that kind of open relationship.' I heard my voice sounding not so sure about that, though. I wondered if the Jack Daniels might have something to do with it.

'What do you two get up to in bed, then?' Mick asked, pulling me towards him by the shoulder for a second, then relaxing his grip. There was a mischievous smile on his face, and the little curled mouse in his trousers was no longer curled or mouse-size, but weasel-long and slender – and straight.

Had it not been for the Jack Daniel's I'd have been shocked by the question. As it was, I took it easily enough. Actually, though, had it not been for the Jack Daniel's Mick probably wouldn't have asked.

'Oh, very basic,' I said. 'Mostly we wank each other. Sometimes we lie tummy to tummy and give our cocks a belly-rub. I learnt that from Giles, by the way.'

Mick laughed, though very nicely. 'Maybe he and I could teach you one or two more new tricks.'

'I suppose you two fuck each other,' I said, trying for a candid, matter-of-fact tone of voice.

'We do that, yes,' Mick said. 'We also suck each other sometimes.'

'Blow-jobs.' I said. I'd heard of that at least. 'Do you actually blow, though?' I asked him.

'No,' he answered, and you don't really have to suck, actually, unless you want to. You just move your head back and forth, or he pushes in and out a bit, and use your lips like you would your fist. But you'd be surprised at the difference in the sensation if you've never done it before.' His hand had dropped down my back, had stolen round my waist and was inching down my groin towards my now hard and painfully bent-under dick. Mick said, 'Do you know what sixty-nine is?'

I said, no, I did not.

He said, 'Well, you can imagine...'

By now I'd caught sight of Cocker. He'd looked up at me, wanting to catch my eye, and had caught it easily, as he always did. Giles's hand was exploring Cocker's thigh, the way it had explored mine a quarter of a year ago. Cocker now gave a little jerk of head and eyes towards the door. I got the message.

'Well, OK, thanks, guys,' I said. 'It's been really great. But we really should be going now.'

We shed our friends' hands and arms as we stood up, the way ducks shed water as they take flight.

'Come again,' said Giles, unabashed.

'And we'll talk about the article as soon as,' said Mick.

We exchanged email addresses, and walked to the door, parting unhurriedly with smiles on all sides, but no hugs or kisses.

Cocker and I walked back a bit silently. Then, as we walked along Walton Street under the lamps, Cocker asked, 'Do you know what sixty-nine is?'

I said, 'Funny you should ask that. No I don't. I was going to ask you.'

'No worries,' he said. 'When we get back we can look it up on the internet.'

Anthony McDonald

SIXTEEN

We found it on Wikipedia – which sounds like an interesting sexual practice in itself. Wikipedia told us nothing we didn't know. We just hadn't previously matched up all the words we knew with all the activities we knew about. We didn't know why we hadn't done this before, we told each other – I mean, look this sort of thing up on the net. No doubt most kids did. Neither of us had an elder brother, though. Perhaps that had something to do with it.

The other thing we hadn't done before – or one other thing at any rate – was to try and take the other's cock in mouth. That had something to do with our determination, a couple of months back, not to identify ourselves as gay. We knew that cocksucker was used in America as a term of abuse, just as gay was. But recent events and declarations had pushed us beyond that.

We didn't stay long online. Better uses for our time were crowding into our thoughts. I dropped to the floor at Cocker's feet, while he stayed sitting at my computer chair. (We were using my room tonight.) I undid his jeans and pulled them down, dragging them and his underpants out from under his buttocks with a little help from him. I found him half erect and very wet.

I shouldered my way between his naked knees and bowed my head into his crotch. I picked him up gently, the way a dog picks up a bird, and felt him swell and stiffen rapidly inside my mouth.

Cocker's reaction was like an electric shock. 'Oh fuck!' he said. 'Wow. Oh hey!' His hands rubbed frantically at the back of my head. I heard my hair crackle. 'This is just so wonderful. So good.'

If it was as wonderful as that, then I wanted a piece of it. I slipped my mouth off him in order to speak. 'Come on. Let's get in bed.'

We got up and undressed ourselves completely. Cocker said, watching me do this, 'God, your pants are wet.'

'Pot calling kettle black,' I said. 'I felt yours when I took them off.'

Cocker got into bed first. I think he did that deliberately. It meant he could have the pillow under his head. I arranged myself on top of him, bending my knees to accommodate the unyielding bed-head. Then we got on with it.

Cocker was right. It was wonderful. More than wonderful. We'd been crazy not to do this before. It seemed so obvious. So right.

Even so, as it was our first crack at this, we had a bit to learn, the two of us. We both gagged a couple of times, so had to disengage and start from scratch. The other thing was that we hadn't negotiated in advance the issue of whether to swallow or not. By the time you each have a cock in your mouth it's physically impossible to discuss it.

Events overtook us rapidly. I shot very suddenly, filling Cocker's mouth. A second later he got his own back: my own mouth was filled with his sweet, salty ejaculate. There was nothing to be done but swallow it: I didn't want to spit it out all over the sheets.

Gamely I gulped and gulped while Cocker pumped to a stop. The same thing seemed to be happening at the other end of me. Then at the same moment we each released the other's cock.

'Blimey,' I heard Cocker say. 'That was an experience and a half.'

I wriggled quickly round until we lay together, me still on top of him, but face to face now, cock to cock.

'We should have talked about the swallowing bit in advance,' I said.

'Hmm,' said Cocker. 'I was OK with it in the end. But next time I might give that bit a miss.'

'I'll free my mouth up and tell you when I'm coming next time. This time it just crept up on me. Sorry about that.'

'Ditto and ditto,' Cocker said.

I put my hand down and caught his slippery, still stiff penis. I started to massage it.

'You can keep doing that,' he said. 'I think it might be ready to go again in a few minutes.'

I felt Cocker's fingers clasp my own dick. 'Mine too,' I said.

I wrote an actual letter to my parents. Sometimes things are too serious for anything else. I explained in it that I'd meant what I said about loving Cocker. That he loved me back. I said the college had divided us by giving us separate rooms, but that they couldn't tear our hearts apart. I didn't mention our new sleeping arrangements. They could guess, if they chose to, or else not. I said when we graduated in two and a half years' time, we'd want a civil partnership.

I composed that letter with Cocker in the room beside me. He read it over very carefully and approved of it. 'Wow,' he said. I added, *PS Cocker sends his best wishes,* then I sealed it, put a stamp on it, and together we walked to the mail-box on the corner of Gloucester Street and posted it.

James had held auditions and assembled his cast of actors. Rehearsals for Journey's End began the following week. All of us were males. The play was set in the Flanders trenches of 14-18, and there were no women there, of course. Most of the young soldiers are presented in the play as stoical and brave but there is one exception. He's a young officer called Hibbert, and he's working at getting invalided out of danger by exaggerating the symptoms of neuralgia from which he suffers.

The young chap playing Hibbert seemed very nice. He was slender and fey-looking, with very light blue eyes, quite long blond hair and a wispy little blond beard that was really cute. He looked at me quite often, I noticed, and he smiled whenever he did that. His name was Ed.

James told him, 'The beard will have to go, I'm afraid, when we actually do it.' He turned to the rest of us. 'And all of you will need short hair when the time comes. Maybe a few hair-cuts.'

James, we couldn't help noticing, hadn't continued to keep his head shaved. His hair had begun to grow back in the last week. He looked marginally better as a result. I mentioned this to Will – who was playing 'Uncle', partly on my recommendation – during a break. 'That's because I told him to,' said Will, grinning. 'I said his shaved head didn't suit him. It made him look ridiculous.'

'Oh wow,' I said. I was impressed. It seemed that Will was a guy who would tell the emperor he had no clothes. He was the mouse (though a very chunky, six-foot, broad-shouldered mouse) who would bell the cat.

Ed came up and spoke to me. 'It's great to meet you,' he said. 'You and Cocker too.' For a moment I couldn't get my head round the cockatoo, but then I sorted it. 'You're kind of famous, I guess.'

Famous? I hadn't really thought of that. 'I don't know about famous,' I said.

He smiled very prettily at me. 'Well, at least you're sort of heroes among gay people here. Everyone knows about the Hamlet review, and what happened at dinner in your college that night.'

The university was a very small world, I thought. 'You probably don't know the next bit,' I told him. I recited the 'Pip rogers Cocker Davis' story: the way the names on our door had been reversed. He laughed and said, 'I think that's really cute.' Then James called us to attention and brought us back to the scene we were working on. 'Tell you more later,' I told Ed as we moved off. 'Drinks at The White Rabbit afterwards.'

The first rehearsal was more of a read-through than anything else. Will was excellent as 'Uncle' Osbourne. I thought I was pretty good as Raleigh actually. As for Cocker, he was just himself. Cocker simply became Captain Stanhope and that was that. At the end of rehearsal James took me aside to give me a private 'note'. 'Don't act so much,' he told me. 'This isn't Hamlet. Take a leaf out of Cocker's book. Just be yourself.'

For a second I felt stung, as if by a tiny unseen insect, but then immediately I realised that James was right. I was the one who people said could be a pro actor, Cocker was not. Yet it was the simple artlessness of Cocker's performance as Horatio that had moved people at least as much as my Hamlet had done, and had touched their hearts. And now I'd been told to take a leaf out of my friend's book. I told James I would do exactly that. I would do it (I didn't tell James this bit) in a spirit of humility and gratitude and love.

We walked round the corner to the White Rabbit, and everybody got a pint. I made a point of getting hold of Ed again and introducing him to Cocker properly. 'The other name on the door,' Ed said. Cocker looked puzzled.

'I've told Ed about the reversal of our names on the door that time,' I explained. 'He already knew about what happened in hall that night.'

'Uhuh,' said Cocker.

I wanted to say, I think Ed's another one of us, but with him standing there I obviously could not.

Ed helped us all out. 'It's nice meeting you two – especially nice for me, I mean – because I think I may be gay but I'm not sure yet.'

Cocker pricked up his ears at that. Had either of us been alone and single, it would have been the cue to give Ed a hug and start on our own researches. *I think I may be gay but I'm not sure yet* is one of the nicest challenges that a gay man more certain of his orientation can pick up. It's certainly a challenge that no unattached gay man – and probably not many attached ones also – can resist.

'I don't think even Cocker's sure about himself yet,' I said. It was the first time I'd dared to make a joke at his expense in public. I wasn't sure how it would go down with him. I looked at him sideways. He seemed OK with it.

It turned out he was more than OK with it. 'That was before I met you, Ed,' he said. 'Now I'm in no more doubt.' It was the first time I'd heard Cocker speak flirtatiously to anyone. I'd never heard him do it even to me. I was a bit startled by it. Today's lesson in love, perhaps.

'Sad to say,' I told Ed, 'we no longer share a room together.' I told him the story of what had happened.

'Oh, no. That's dreadful,' he said.

Cocker said, 'A friend of ours is thinking of writing a newspaper article about it.'

I chipped in, 'He's the person who wrote that review of Hamlet that started it all.'

'Oh, he's a friend of yours?' Ed said.

Cocker said rather hurriedly, 'No, no. That sounds bad like that. He wasn't a friend when he wrote the article. We've met him since. Actually just last week.'

Well, we'd first met Mick in the club after the first night, but I wasn't going to bring that up. Cocker was giving an outline of the situation, not every detail in the case.

I turned to Cocker. 'We ought to introduce Ed to Mick and Giles,' I said. 'Take him round one night.'

Cocker looked back at me. 'Are you mad?' he said, then laughed.

I laughed too, and then Ed laughed, though he was clearly wondering, if perhaps half guessing, what the laugh was about. 'Why do you say that?' Ed asked.

Cocker answered. 'Because the two of them tried to make the two of us when we went round to theirs last week.'

'I see,' said Ed. 'A kind of foursome. It sounds rather interesting actually.'

'Perhaps we should send Ed round there on his own,' I said naughtily.

Cocker said, 'Well, you first went there on your own...'

'Before I really knew you...' I interrupted.

But Cocker continued smoothly, 'And look at him now.' This was addressed to Ed.

'I think you'll have to give me that address,' Ed said with a giggle.

Was it my imagination, or were the three of us all being a little camp?

A letter arrived from my parents. I needed Cocker with me when I opened it. I had to steel myself.

Darling Pip,

You're obviously serious about Cocker. And at 18, of course you're grown up and can do what you like.

Daddy and I were a bit shocked, actually, to see you writing about a civil partnership with someone you've known such a short time, and when you're both so young and, in your case at least, not very experienced in matters of the heart.

But then we thought about what you wrote next. You talked of giving things till the end of your Oxford career before having a civil partnership. We thought that was sensible of you, and right.

If you and Cocker are still as serious about that idea in two years' time as you seem to be now, we'd give the partnership idea our blessing. Though we'd both beg you not to consider a commitment like that to someone of your own sex before that.

Just don't rush into things is all we're saying. And in the meantime, please invite Cocker to come and stay with us in Oare for as big a chunk of the Easter vacation as you want. Send him our fondest wishes.

With all my love

Mummy

I nearly cried with relief. So did Cocker, actually. He'd read it over my shoulder, clasping my hand to give me support.

'I think that's wonderful,' Cocker said.

'So do I, sort of,' I said. 'But it does sort of say they wouldn't give their blessing to a partnership if we wanted one – or needed one – before that. It's also a bit... I mean … *a commitment like that to someone of your own sex* … like, if you were a girl they'd be happy for us to tie the knot today?'

'Give them a chance,' said Cocker, suddenly mature and wise. 'They've had a lot to take in very suddenly. They'll need a bit of time to digest it. And anyway,' he squeezed my shoulder, 'don't look a gift horse in the mouth.'

SEVENTEEN

An email came from Mick the next day. He had been given the go-ahead to do an article about our case – the room-share thing, that is – and had a draft ready for us to look at. Would we like to pop round one evening soon and discuss it?

The sooner the better seemed the obvious answer to that. But this evening I had rehearsals, though for once Cocker did not. We said we'd go along tomorrow. We added cheekily that we'd be wearing underpants.

The rehearsal that evening went well. At the end of it there were just Ed and me left. Well, there was James, directing us, obviously. But he wanted to go straight back to his college afterwards. This left me and Ed together out on the pavement of Beaumont Street. Neither of us wanted to part at that moment, I discovered. Ed said to me a bit bashfully, 'Do you want to go for a drink?' We had never done such a thing together as 'just the two of us'.

I thought quickly. 'I'd like to,' I said. 'I'll just text Cocker. See if he wants to join us.'

I typed, *In white rabbit with ed. Join us?*

He answered with a call. 'Yeah,' he said. 'I'm nearly finished with this essay. I'll be there in fifteen if that's OK? I love you, Cockerfuckerpip.'

'Love you, Cockerfuckercocker,' I said. 'See you in a bit.'

Ed said, with a sheen of delighted astonishment in his voice, 'Is that what you call him?!'

'Yeah,' I said. 'You probably weren't meant to hear that.' Actually I was happy he'd heard that. 'He calls me Cockerfuckerpip.'

I think that little bit of info had excited Ed. He said, while we were still crossing the yard to the pub, 'And do you? Do you two actually fuck?'

I stopped walking. It wasn't a conversation we could be having as we strolled in at the front door of The White Rabbit and marched up to the bar. 'Actually, no,' I said. 'It's something we've never done yet.'

'Do you want to?' Ed asked.

'I think so,' I said. 'I'm not quite sure, though.' I looked at him carefully. 'Have you ever done it?' I thought I knew what the answer would be to that.

'No,' he said, a bit shyly. I'd been right.

'With a girl, though?'

'I've never fucked anyone yet.'

To put him at his ease I said, 'Neither have I. Nor has Cocker. We've never fucked anyone of either sex, and neither of us has ever been fucked.'

Ed grinned at me. 'Join the club,' he said.

'Join ours,' I said.

We resumed our interrupted walk and went on into the pub. But when we had got our pints and sat at one of the tables in a rather dark corner, where the little candle on the table flickered shadows over us, we went back to our conversation. It was too good an opportunity, for both of us, not to take.

I told Ed in some detail the history of my sexual experience with Cocker and he lapped it up. I told him how we enjoyed masturbating each other, how we'd added belly-rubbing our cocks after I'd first done that lying on top of Giles's tummy, and how in just the last few days we'd started sucking each other off. I asked him if he'd heard of sixty-nine, and he had. 'I've heard of just about everything. Only I've never done anything with anyone. Only with myself, so to speak.'

'Well, getting sucked is lovely,' I said.

He cut me off. 'I do know that,' he said. 'I'm very flexible. I can suck myself. I do it from time to time when I want to cheer myself up.'

The idea of all that sent a delicious thrill through me. Of course I wanted to see him do that. I said, 'Do you … you know … do you come in your own mouth?'

'Occasionally,' he said. 'Usually by accident.' He gave me a broad and lovely smile across the table. 'Bet you can't do that.'

'You're right. I can't,' I said. 'Neither can Cocker. As far as I know I've never met anyone who could.' Do I say it or don't I? I asked myself. Danger signals flashed. I said it anyway. 'Wouldn't mind seeing you do it, though.'

He said, 'And I wouldn't mind sucking you off.'

Bloody hell! I thought. I'm pretty well a married man, and I'm sitting at a candle-lit table in The White Rabbit with a pretty little elf of a boy and we're talking like this... while waiting for Cocker to turn up.

I felt his left knee shunt my right knee under the table. I returned the pressure, just to let him know I was OK with this.

'You know,' he said. 'I wasn't happy with the idea that I was gay, didn't even want to admit to myself that's what I was, till I met you. Met you and Cocker. You've given me so much confidence. I'm OK with it now.'

'That's great,' I said. 'All you need now is to find your own boyfriend.'

'I guess you're right,' he said thoughtfully. 'But I can't help wishing I could do it with you and Cocker first.'

The novel thought of this lit me up like a firework for a moment. I even visualised, in a flash, the positions we would all adopt. But I did think, caution. Society tends to believe two is company, three's a crowd, when it comes to long-term relationships. I guessed there was some good reason for that, though I couldn't imagine at that moment what the reason was. 'I'm not sure if Cocker would go along with that,' I said, choosing the coward's way out.

'Wonderful name, Cocker,' Ed said. 'Is he called that because he's got a big cock?'

'Not really,' I told him. 'It's a tiny bit bigger than mine is, but not very much.'

'That doesn't tell me much,' he said. 'I don't know how big yours is. For all I know you may be huge.'

I laughed and said, 'I'm not.'

I was pretty well inflated at that moment though, within the confines of my pants. Just then I felt Ed's hand dart like a mouse along my thigh, and score a bull's-eye when it came to guessing the location of my dick.

I didn't stop to reason with myself but, leaning across and under the table, just as he was, ran my own hand from his knee to his crotch and grabbed his cock. Which was in the same state as mine was. As far as I could tell through the denim, we were the same size, more or less.

'You're just like me,' he said. 'That's nice.'

Thank God we were tucked around the corner from the bar. We heard Cocker's voice say hallo to someone as he came in through the door... Before we could see him or, more importantly, before he could see us.

Ed and I shot backwards from each other like magnets whose polarity is suddenly reversed. 'Cocker,' I called, loudly and brightly. 'We're round here.'

His head appeared around the edge of the door-jamb. 'Just getting myself a pint.' His head disappeared again.

I didn't feel I'd been in any way unfaithful to him. But I found I'd done enough to feel guilty about. It was another of those lessons in love.

There would be an atmosphere around our table that Cocker would pick up on as soon as he joined us. It would be – for him – like entering a room in which someone has just farted, but you don't know who. I knew I'd have to dispel it by saying something he wouldn't expect to hear. Cocker appeared again a few seconds later, carrying his pint glass. He arrived at our table. Even before he had pulled out the chair he was going to sit on I said, 'Ed's joining us when we go to Giles's tomorrow night.'

'Oh,' Cocker said. Then he flashed me a grin and flashed Ed another one. 'Well, that'll be nice. Last time there were just the four of us and it got a bit intense.'

Ed raised his glass and said, 'Cheers,' to Cocker, then Cocker and I said 'Cheers.' Ed hadn't batted an eyelid in response to my improvised ad lib. He was a good little actor, was Ed. I still felt a bit bad at what had taken place, but as we all began to talk amiably of other things I began to feel better about it.

We met Ed outside our own college at the bottom of Beaumont Street, and walked as a trio to Giles's house. We were given a warm welcome by Giles and Mick. As on the last occasion we'd been there they were dressed in very lightweight clothes, and the heating was turned up pleasantly high. Our hosts seemed especially pleased to see Ed.

Giles told us that his amateur theatre group were going to do The Importance of Being Earnest by Oscar Wilde. It had just been decided. Giles had been cast as Jack Worthing and Mick was to play Algernon. We promised we would all go and see it. In their turn they promised us they would come and see Journey's End when we presented it in a few weeks' time. Then Giles poured all of us a Jack Daniels.

Cocker and I sat on one of the two sofas, Ed sat on the other one, facing us, and sandwiched between Giles and Mick. It looked quite a tight squeeze, though a pleasant one – if that was what the three of them wanted.

Mick had already handed a couple of sheets of paper to Cocker. They were a printout of the article he had drafted for the local press. Cocker and I held it between us and we read it together.

We thought he'd been quite clever. He had written about the fact that one of the colleges had deliberately separated a couple to whom they had given a shared room at the start of the academic year. They had been split up only when it had come to the notice of the college authorities that the two people in question had actually started living as a couple.

But what did living as a couple mean? Mick's article had gone on. Since nobody had snooped on the two people in the privacy of their own bedroom, nor had the two in question volunteered anything on the subject, it could only be that the college had acted on information that was no more than an assumption based on hearsay.

Towards the end of the article there was a one-line quote from Cocker on the subject and one from me. We were named. Cocker Davis, although having an unusual name, could be presumed to be a man, but Pip Rogers could have been the name of a person of either sex. Some readers of the article would know me, of course, and some might remember that I'd played Hamlet the previous term. But the point had been made. Only in the last paragraph did Mick reveal the fact that the couple he was writing about were two blokes. He then asked readers, rhetorically, whether that new knowledge made any difference to the opinions they had formed as they read through the article. And if it did make a difference … then what were the implications of that?

Cocker and I approved of Mick's article whole-heartedly. 'Brilliant, Mick,' Cocker said. Then he handed the papers over to Ed so that he could satisfy his own curiosity.

'Glad you like it,' Mick said, and Giles beamed his satisfaction on his friend's behalf. And when he'd read it through Ed added his own approval to the consensus, and received a light pat on the leg from Mick by way of thanks.

Either that pat on the leg or the Jack Daniels – he was on his second glass – loosened Ed's tongue. He began to ask the older two about themselves as a couple. Where and how had they first met? How long had they been together?

'Together is a funny word,' Giles said. 'It means different things to different people. In our case – Mick's and mine – I'd say we were kind of semi-detached. We're anchored together, if you like, but we consider ourselves free to see other people and do different things. It suits us both.'

'Which makes it OK,' Mick chipped in. 'Because that's what both of us want. It's only if one of you likes it that way and the other doesn't that things go wrong. There are couples and couples, though.' He hesitated. I could see him wondering whether or not to refer to Cocker and me.

Giles did it for him. He knew us better than Mick did. Knew me much better, especially; neither of us had forgotten that dick-on-belly rub. Giles said, 'Some couples are special, though. I think those two may be a case in point. I think they have an exclusivity clause in their contract.' He looked across at us and grinned. 'Am I right?'

'Never really thought about it,' Cocker said airily. 'Never needed to. We're just us. It's always just the two of us.' He made it sound so simple. Perhaps it was.

As time passed I could see the sort of things happening on the sofa opposite us that had happened between Giles and Cocker, and between Mick and me, last time we'd been here. Arms were going around necks, and pats on legs were exchanged among the three of them. Ed seemed more than happy with the amount of attention he was getting from the older pair. I wondered a little about what would happen next, though really I knew perfectly well, and of course it did. Cocker squeezed my thigh and said, 'Reckon it's time for home? What d'ya think?'

I was a little bit torn, but only a little bit. Group sex involving maybe all five of us would have been an exciting experience. And I really would have liked to see Ed sucking his own prick. (That was something I hadn't yet told Cocker about.) But I wanted Cocker more than I wanted that. I wanted to be alone with him. Just the two of us, snuggled together for the rest of ever. I didn't want anything else. 'Yeah,' I said. 'Time to head back, perhaps.'

Cocker said, 'You coming, Ed? Or staying put for a bit?' He said it in a very even tone, giving Ed the chance to come away at the same time as we did without it looking awkward, if that was what he wanted to do, but at the same time not forcing it.

'You don't need to go yet if you don't want to,' Giles said. He might have been talking to the three of us, but the remark could equally well have been interpreted as being addressed simply to Ed.

Ed took his cue. 'I might stay on with these guys a little longer,' he said. He gave a little wag of shoulders and head. 'If they're sure that's all right.

They all got up and walked with us to the door, though, and we said very friendly goodnights. We all kissed one another, Cocker and I even kissing Ed.

As we walked back from Jericho and into Walton Street, Cocker said, 'Ed may have been uncertain whether he's gay or not until recently. But I think he may be going to find out tonight.'

'In good company, at least,' I said. 'He'll be pretty safe.'

'How do you mean?' Cocker asked.

'I mean – well – whatever happens, they'll be gentle with him. They won't do anything he doesn't want. I'm sure of that. That's the way Giles was with me, at any rate. He said as much, and behaved accordingly.'

'Yep. I see,' said Cocker. 'I wouldn't want to think we'd left him with people who'd tie him up, gang-bang him and leave him for dead.'

'Bloody hell, mate,' I said. 'You're giving me the creeps.'

'You know,' said Cocker, sounding as if was changing to a more serious tack. 'We never talked about being exclusive… I mean, not until Giles mentioned it. But we sort of are, aren't we? Isn't that what we're about? Not like Giles and Mick. Not like Ed.'

'That's what I want,' I said. A thought surfaced suddenly. It was a heavy one. One I wasn't comfortable with. 'I suppose I ought to tell you this,' I said.

'Oh,' said Cocker. 'I suppose that if you suppose you ought to, then you ought. Though I guess I'm not going to like it.'

'You probably won't,' I said. 'Though I hope you won't think it's as bad as all that.'

'We'll see,' said Cocker grimly, and my heart sank.

I took a breath and hoped for the best. 'When we were in the pub last night, before you arrived, Ed and I were talking about this and that. Including the size of our cocks.'

'What?!' said Cocker incredulously. 'You were talking to someone else about the size of your cock? And his?'

'Well…'

'And did mine get a mention by any chance?' Cocker said in his coldest tone of voice. I'd heard that tone only rarely, but whenever I had done it had filled me with dismay and dread.

I sighed involuntarily. I said, 'Only in passing… We were just larking around. Look, I'll finish this up. Just for a joke – and only for a joke – we both reached under the table and touched each other's through our jeans.

There was nothing more to it than that. I just thought I ought to tell you that.'

'There was nothing more to it than that because I arrived at that moment,' Cocker said flatly. 'I did wonder what you'd been talking about…' He thought for a second, then added, 'And were you both stiff?'

'Yes,' I admitted. 'Not fully, but a little bit.' I had understated this slightly, but decided that, even so, I'd said enough. 'Sorry, Cocker,' I said. 'I now feel totally wretched… Now I've talked about it to you. It's made it all seem much bigger, somehow, and much worse.'

'And I feel totally wretched too,' said Cocker, 'now you've told me that. Don't know if that makes you feel better.'

'No, it doesn't,' I said. The words came out angrily. I surprised myself. 'Of course it doesn't. Don't get sarky with me, please.'

'And don't you go grabbing other blokes' cocks,' he said, his own voice rising as he spoke. 'At least I don't do that.' He paused a second. Then, 'I really hated hearing you tell me that.'

'Do you wish I hadn't told you, then?' I asked.

He seemed unsure for a moment how to answer that. In the end he said, 'I only wish you hadn't touched his cock.'

I could have said, *Me too,* but I didn't. Anger had gone in an instant. Anguish was in its place. I said very quietly, 'I love you,' instead.

'I love you too,' he said, equally quietly. His voice was full of tears.

We hugged each other then and there, on the corner of Walton Street and Beaumont Street. And then, heedless of who might see us, we both broke down and wept.

EIGHTEEN

It couldn't have been better.

Though there was a moment when it couldn't have been worse. There was a moment – it was the moment when Cocker and I said we both felt totally wretched – when I felt my life was in free-fall. That I was dropping without a parachute and would be dashed to pieces and oblivion on the ground. That life wasn't worth living any more. I felt as though I was already dead and burning up in hell. I'd thought that we wouldn't share a bed that night. That we'd return separately to our cold beds in different buildings. That that would be only the start of it.

But what a difference a declaration of love makes. In the middle of the street outside the college we sobbed our hearts out in each other's arms. The only words we had were our *I love yous* repeated a hundred times. Then we pulled ourselves together, pulled ourselves apart, and walked side by side towards the postern gate. We even walked through that together, squeezing side by side. We went up to my room and quickly undressed each other. How beautiful Cocker looked. Naked and erect. I walked him to the mirror and we stood side by side. Cocker said, contemplating our double reflection, 'How beautiful you look. Naked and erect.'

I said, 'You too, mate.'

We embraced again and kissed, forgetful of the mirror that stood watching us. We got into bed. I felt Cocker's fingers come around my hard cock at the same moment as I grasped his. We just held them there for a moment, not yet starting to stroke. I knew that nothing could ever be better than this moment.

Then I heard Cocker say it. 'No moment in my life has been better than this.'

I thought the that if there was such a state as heaven, this is what it would be like. We got down to business and started slowly, as if in a trance or state of enchantment, to wank each other off.

We met Ed the next evening at rehearsals, though I didn't have a chance to talk to him on his own until we were walking across to the pub afterwards. I was walking close alongside him but was careful not to touch him at any point. 'So what happened after we left last night?' I asked him. Though I'd been able to kind of guess from the expression that had appeared in his eyes every time our glances had crossed during rehearsal.

'Quite a lot, actually,' he said. 'We all got naked soon after you left and played with one another's dicks a bit. Giles is massively equipped, by the way.'

'I know that,' I said, a bit brusquely, 'I've played with it myself.' Then I added carefully, 'Though that was before I got it together with Cocker. We're pretty exclusive now. After the subject came up yesterday evening, we talked about that.' But I couldn't resist asking, 'What's Mick's like, though? I've never seen that.'

'Handy household size,' Ed said lightly. 'Like mine and yours. Which I'd still like to see properly one day, incidentally. Anyway, Mick's is cute. We went upstairs eventually and all got into bed. I told them I could suck myself and they asked for a demo, which I did, just for a second or two. Then Mick asked me if he could fuck me. I was a bit scared at the thought but I manned up and said, why not?

'He rolled a condom on, put some KY on his fingers and pushed that up my arse. Then he put his cock in where the fingers had been and it actually felt nice. He lay behind me, his chest against my back. Giles lay in front of me. Face to face and cock to cock. Giles and I wanked each other and…'

We had reached the front door of the pub. Ed wound up his tale quickly. 'Then we all came quite quickly. Mick inside me, Giles and me into each other's pubes. Made a bit of a mess in the bed. Actually I'm going back there again tonight. I get you a pint?'

Two minutes later we were sorted, sitting at a table. I was talking to Will now, but I heard Cocker saying to Ed, 'So, after we left last night…?' I didn't hear Ed's reply to that. Presumably Cocker was regaled with the same story that Ed had told me. We'd be able to compare notes afterwards.

We did compare notes. On the walk back to our college home and bed. It was clear that Ed had told the same story to both of us. There was no reason to doubt him. It was apparent that Ed, for all his previous lack of sexual experience had now had one particular experience that neither Cocker nor I had had. He'd had his arse fucked.

'He didn't say anything about it hurting him,' Cocker said.

'Then it probably didn't. After all, it was Mick who fucked him. Ed said he doesn't have as big a cock as Giles does. That it's only the same size as mine is.'

'Which he knows about because he's felt you up,' Cocker said tersely. I realised I'd got onto wobbly ground. Cocker cautioned, 'I'd rather you didn't keep bringing that up.'

'Sorry, darling,' I said. 'He wore a condom,' I said in an effort to change the subject slightly. 'And used a lube of some sort.'

'We wouldn't need condoms,' Cocker said. 'As neither of us has ever had that sort of sex with anybody else.' He paused. 'I suppose that's still true in your case?'

That hurt, but I didn't protest. I'd deserved Cocker's barb. 'It's true, Cocker. I've never done anything, for good or ill, that you don't know about.' I think it was my practice with Hamlet's speeches that enabled me to come out with fancy phrases like *for good or ill*.

Cocker's reply was by no means fancy or Shakespearean. It took me pleasantly by surprise. 'We can just use spit.'

I had often wondered which of the two of us, when and if the time came, would fuck the other first. I now knew the answer to that. Cocker was clearly going to fuck me before I had a chance to do him first. And he was going to do it tonight.

We went to Cocker's room. We undressed ourselves this time, watching each other closely as we did so but not touching. We both twitched involuntary smiles as our dicks came springing out and up. I registered once again the fact that Cocker's was marginally bigger than mine, both in girth and length. Never mind. What would be would be. He was nowhere near as big as Giles was, and I was grateful for that.

Cocker put his hands on my naked shoulders and we pulled together till our cocks mashed. 'I want to fuck you now,' he said. 'Is that all right? Then you can fuck me any time you like.'

'It's all right,' I said.

'Don't be nervous,' Cocker said softly. 'I'll be very gentle. I promise I won't hurt you.'

Of course that did make me nervous. 'If it does hurt,' I asked a bit anxiously, 'will you stop?'

'Obviously,' Cocker said, nuzzling my ear with his cheek. 'I'd never hurt a hair of your head.'

'It's not the hairs of my head I'm worried about,' I said. We both laughed, then we got into bed.

I lay on my back, the way I did – or Cocker did – when we rubbed off on each other's belly. I spread my legs and let Cocker shunt himself between them. 'I've seen this done on videos,' he admitted a bit bashfully.

'So have I,' I told him equally shyly. We'd neither of us told the other that.

He knelt up between my legs, letting the duvet fall down his back. Then he spat on his hand and started to spread it around his dick. He spat again on the fingers of his other hand and then very gently worked one finger into my hole and a little way up. At first it felt very tight and tense. But then I realised I rather liked it. I clutched my own dick and started to work it. And then, very gently, very smoothly, Cocker drew his finger out, then re-inserted it. He started to do this again and again. I felt myself growing more and more relaxed.

Cocker said, 'I'll put it in now if you're OK with that.' I simply nodded and grunted, and Cocker did exactly as he'd said. It felt like a moistened finger again, but one that was three times as big as most people's fingers are. Then there we were: Cocker fucking me, and me being fucked.

We relaxed into it, the pair of us. We abandoned ourselves to the moment. Cocker pulled my bottom into the air a little way and I wrapped my legs around his shoulders like a scarf. After a couple more minutes Cocker announced, 'Oh man, I'm coming.' His thrusts grew manic and I felt him swell and pulse inside me. He seemed to go on shooting for ever. Then he collapsed on top of my chest.

A minute later he raised his torso off me again and started work on my very hard cock with his hand. His cock was also very hard. It was still inside me. I came in floods a minute later, dousing my chest and speckling my throat. The sensation was vast and wonderful. But there was a small pique of disappointment attached to this, as there is to every sublime human experience. It meant that I wouldn't be getting my cock into Cocker for a little while yet.

But… I didn't have to be patient for too long. I awoke during the night to find myself lying on my side and curled around Cocker spoon-wise, my again rigid cock pressed up against his peachy behind. I reached round and grabbed his cock, which was also erect and strong. I didn't pause to think too much. I moistened my dick with spit and shoved it into his buttock cleft and hoped for the best. It found its goal first time, and slid in, like a sword into its scabbard, up to the hilt. Cocker was as relaxed as it was possible to be, being fast asleep. I started gently to thrust into him, at the same time pulling his cock back and forth.

Cocker woke up slowly, into the gradual awareness that he was being fucked for the first time in his life. I wondered what he would say when he started to speak. He said sleepily, 'Go for it, baby.' So I did. When I came I felt as though my life blood was pouring out of me into Cocker. That, along with my love I was making a present to him of my life. When he came, a half minute afterwards, he soaked the sheets.

'How do you feel?' I asked him in the morning.

'What? You mean physically? Around my arse? Or generally. Spiritually.'

'Both,' I said.

'Good on all counts,' he answered. 'Slightly sore, perhaps…'

'I know,' I said. 'It's a bit like when you've had a very hot curry the night before and you go to the bog.'

'Well put,' he said, and gave me a grin across the small space in which we were getting dressed.

'We'll do it again, though, won't we?' I checked.

'You bet we will,' he said. 'And probably tonight. Pip rogers Cocker and Cocker rogers Pip.'

'You're on,' I said. But I bent down to tie my laces at that point, and that gave me a twinge, I must admit.

We'd given no thought, oddly enough, to the two guys who now shared what had been our double room in our first term. Someone had told us they were two men in their third year. We didn't know what their names were and we hadn't gone up their staircase to look. But now their existence and the ramifications of their existence were brought to our attention by – of all people – Ed.

He greeted us at rehearsal that day with an announcement. 'There's a development in your case. The newspaper article Mick's doing, I mean. He said he's contacted the two guys who share your room. Apparently they both feel a bit awkward about it. Actually, although they get on OK, they'd prefer to have single rooms again. They've both got girlfriends and so it's a bit… Well, you know.'

'Interesting,' I said, thinking that was that.

But Ed had more to say. 'They've said they're prepared to talk to the newspaper, after the article has appeared, in a follow-up interview with Mick. They're prepared to stick their necks out and say you were badly treated and that they'd be the first to wish you well in your efforts to get your old room back.' That all came out in one breath. I was pretty sure that Ed had memorised the words that had been said to him by Mick. Then Ed said, 'The other thing is that I had my first active fuck last night.'

'Oh,' said Cocker. He was unable to pretend he wasn't interested in this. 'Who did you…?'

'I did Mick. From behind, while he lay across the bed, kneeling on the floor. Giles watched, sitting cross-legged on the bed and playing with his dick a bit. Then Mick fucked Giles, while I watched.'

Cocker grinned. 'Good on yer, mate. Actually I fucked Pip last night, curiously enough. And he fucked me. Not telling you who went first. And nobody watched.'

I read a message to me in that. Cocker had told Ed everything he wanted Ed to know about our most recent adventure in bed and love. He didn't want me spilling any further details. I took careful note.

We decided that discretion was the better part of valour. We didn't attempt to fuck each other that night. We were both a bit sore still. But our cocks were in perfect shape, and we played with those with great enthusiasm and abandon until we both came explosively, then went to sleep in each other's arms. We went to sleep in love.

In the morning Mick's article appeared in the newspaper and all hell broke loose.

A note arrived from the master of the college to say that he wanted to see us. There was a message from the representative of the UK Union of Students, offering support and any guidance we needed. There was a phone-call from Mick. One of the national newspapers had shown an interest in the case. Would we like to talk about this? In the meantime we both had to go, separately, to our morning lectures and run the gauntlet of the comments and curiosity of our tutors and our peers.

In fact that proved good for us. Explaining the situation and what we felt about it was like a rehearsal for what was to come. We prepared our heads for the possibility of supping with the devil: or getting into bed, so to speak, with the national press. We braced ourselves for a second and perhaps less friendly interview with the master of our college, and we tried to think how we'd respond to the UK Union of Students.

The second good thing to come out of those chats with our lecture group peers was the discovery that they were without exception well-disposed towards us. That might not be the case when we had to confront the master, or face the fickle and unpredictable attentions of the media – if we decided to do that – but it was a start, at least.

NINETEEN

The master poured the Tio Pepe sherry affably enough, and we sat down on one of his sofas this second time. As before, we were distracted, almost overwhelmed by finding ourselves in a room hung with tapestries. They do tend to take you out of your day to day experience of life. Perhaps that is the purpose of tapestries; perhaps it always was.

'Why go to the press?' was his opening line, once he'd sat down in the armchair opposite. 'I gave you the opportunity to come back and have a further chat with me. An opportunity you did not take. Instead you went to the press.'

'We didn't go to the press,' I said. 'The press came to us.'

'That might be a technicality,' the master said. 'The fact remains that you agreed to talk to them.' He picked up a copy of the newspaper in question and waved it as if it were a conductor's baton and he were cueing an orchestra to start. 'You are quoted verbatim in this report.'

Cocker spoke up. 'The journalist in question told us you'd be invited to put your side of the case. We thought we'd find a verbatim quote from yourself.'

'I declined to comment,' the master said. 'As you should have done. This was, and still remains, a college matter. It should have been resolved internally, in the Oxford college spirit.' He smiled. 'And I'm sure it still can be.'

'Resolving it, as far as Mr Davis and I are concerned,' I said, 'would mean giving us our old room back. Are you saying you'd be prepared to do that?'

The master smiled even more urbanely. 'I think you know that I wouldn't be able to go as far as that. But I can see a possible compromise that I think might suit. I think it would not be beyond the realms of possibility to find the pair of you a couple of rooms on the same staircase. Perhaps adjacent rooms on the top floor of the staircase. You wouldn't find yourselves disturbed very much.'

I thought about this. It seemed quite an attractive compromise. It would be like sharing a flat in effect. Our own suite. We wouldn't have a double bed, of course, but then we hadn't had one of those in our original room. I think that had I been alone at that moment I would meekly have said yes to this. But I couldn't. Cocker was a part of this, and I needed to know how he felt.

I looked at him, but he was resolutely showing his profile to me, while looking the master in the face. I was getting good at reading Cocker's mind, but I did need to look into his eyes – those blue seeing-stones of his – to know the contents of his head and heart.

But I heard him speak just then. To the master. He said, 'And that offer would be effective from what date?'

'From the start of next term,' the master replied smoothly.

We were barely halfway through the current term. Oxford was still in winter's frosty grip. The start of next term was months away. Leaves would be green on the trees, and summer would be at hand. It was an unimaginable length of time to look ahead. I no longer needed to see Cocker's eyes to know his thoughts. I voiced them myself.

'That's far too long to wait,' I said. 'You must know that. You must know what it is to be in love!'

'That,' said the master, 'is a question which, even in indirect form, is never asked of one gentleman by another.'

I had to confess, to myself at least, that he was probably right about that. I didn't say so, though. In a negotiation you don't.

'Sorry,' I heard Cocker say, 'but I agree with Mr Rogers. Next term just isn't soon enough. Thank you for the offer, though.'

The master took a sip of sherry. So did Cocker, so did I. It was better than the one my parents served. I made a mental note to tell them that.

'Then I have to lay the following possibilities out,' the master said. 'You may contact the press again and distance yourself from the opinions expressed in the article, explaining that the matter is an internal, college one. Otherwise I shall be forced to take the matter up with the college governing body and hold discussions about your futures as members of this college. In that case you would in due course hear from us.' He stood up. 'I hope it doesn't come to that. I look forward to reading your revised views in the press in the very near future.'

We stood up. The interview was ended. We all shook hands but without much in the way of friendliness. Under the cloak of smooth words the master had threatened to send us down. To end our university careers. To scupper our chances of getting our degrees from Oxford. It might make the world of difference to our financial futures. To say nothing of what our parents would say and think…

As we walked away from the master's lodging, too shocked for the moment to find speech, my mind's eye was filled with beautiful tapestries, with forest scenes and lions and unicorns, and white-robed maidens, and I thought what an unreal and unpredictable thing the life of this world was.

A meeting was in progress. We were in Giles's house, though Giles wasn't there. Mick was, as was the representative of the UK Students' Union. Then there were Cocker and me and – a surprise, this – the two guys who now occupied our old room. Though they were in their third year they turned out to be approachable, fun, and nice. They were also a pretty hearty pair. One rowed for the college, the other captained its Rugby team.

'I think,' said Mick, 'that if the master says it should be kept as a college matter, you should probably take him up on that. Play his game, and beat him at it.'

'Sounds fine,' said Cocker. 'In principle, at least. But exactly how…?'

'I think we could do something about that,' said one of the two guys from our old room. The Rugby captain. He was called Chris. 'We haven't finalised our interview with Mick yet. We could include the idea that it's a college matter, for the moment, at least. And that we're getting up a petition, and a Facebook campaign, to have you reinstated in our – I mean, your – room. The petition and the campaign would be restricted to college members only. We'd actually make a point of saying that…'

'Bet we could get every single college member to sign up,' said his room-mate, the rower Jack. 'You're popular guys, you two. They couldn't rusticate the entire college. They'd be an international laughing stock.'

Mick came back in. 'If they then decided to take no notice of the will of the entire student body, we could reasonably say you had no choice but to go back to the press. This time there'd be no holds barred. We'd get the TV companies and all the nationals…'

'To say nothing of the press in other countries,' said the Union rep. 'Remember, huge numbers of Oxford students come from beyond our shores these days…'

The meeting went on a bit after that, and a certain amount of Jack Daniels went down the hatch. But the main points had been made already. The next thing was to put the new strategy into effect and to see what would happen after that.

Giles returned before the meeting broke up, and with him was Ed. They wanted to know what had been decided, and were pleased with what we told them. After a little while we – that is Cocker and I, and Jack and Chris, and the Union guy, all left. We walked a little way together, before we split at the bottom of Beaumont Street. As we parted it was Chris who asked the question, albeit a bit tentatively. 'Those three. Mick and Giles and Ed. Do they all…?'

'They seem to have become a trio in the last week,' I said.

'Well, good luck to them,' Chris said, and Jack nodded. 'Each to his own. Though I think they might have a bit of trouble getting *that* past the college authorities – of any college – if they wanted a room for three.'

'Just as well that two of them aren't students,' I said. 'They very sensibly confine their activities to the inside of Giles's house.' We all laughed, and the group broke up.

When Cocker and I got back to his room we were feeling vastly more positive than we'd done at the end of our meeting with the master, and the Jack Daniels had had very little to do with that. As we undressed, Cocker put an arm around my waist and rubbed one finger into the cleft between my buttock cheeks. 'Still feeling sore up there?' he queried.

'Not any more,' I said.

'Nor me,' said Cocker brightly. I smiled into his eyes. There wasn't much doubt at that moment as to what we'd be doing when, in just another minute, we climbed together into bed.

The following evening Cocker and I walked together into hall for dinner. It was a formal evening, and we all wore our academic gowns. The master and most of the dons were at high table, similarly dressed. As soon as we appeared there was a drumming of knife handles on tables that was almost deafening. A chorused shout arose. It was so loud and ragged that I couldn't tell what the words were at first. But then I made the words out. 'Give them their room back! Give them their room back!' This was repeated four times, and then the hubbub subsided as quickly as it had arisen.

Neither Cocker nor I attempted to say anything. We both held our hands half up, in a sort of no-comment gesture. I hardly dared to glance at the master. But I did. To my surprise I saw him make a similar gesture as he sat at the centre of the table. For a moment I thought of the Supper at Emmaus painting by Caravaggio, in which Jesus is raising his hands to bless the food. I wondered what the impact of the sudden little demonstration of support for Cocker and me would be. I wondered if the master was wondering the same thing.

Mick's interview with Chris and Jack was a corker. I'd had no previous sight of a draft of it, but read it when it appeared in the paper a couple of days later, just as everyone else in the city and the university did. Chris and Jack were quoted as saying that a person's sexual orientation should not be taken into account when deciding anything in today's world. They said that although there were still places in the world – Russia and parts of Central America and the Middle East got name-checks – where this was regrettably still the case, there was no reason why Oxford, at the forefront of the ongoing enlightenment of the world for the best part of a millennium, should rush backwards to join them.

They went on to say, Jack and Chris did, that they understood that they were commenting on an internal college matter. They explained that they wanted the outside world to know what was going on, but did not require its intervention at this stage. They were confident that a solution would be found within the college itself after reference to the student body. The planned petition was mentioned, and there was a link to the campaign on Facebook.

For the second time in three months I found complete strangers coming up to me and shaking my hand in the street. There were drinks at The Head of the River that night. Giles and Mick. Cocker and me. Chris and Jack and their two girlfriends. Ed, of course. The guy from the Union plus his girlfriend. Will and the rest of the cast of Journey's End. Other people came and joined us…

When Cocker and I awoke in the morning we realised that we not only had headaches. We'd also gone to sleep before we'd even thought about making love.

The petition, and the Facebook page, both began with a disclaimer. They were concerned with one issue only. It was about an individual case. Should the campaign prove successful, the result would not be used as a precedent to be cited in other cases. The floodgates would not be opened for every boyfriend girlfriend pair, or every boyfriend boyfriend pair, or every girlfriend girlfriend pair to demand to share a room in college. In signing the petition, or in signing up to the Facebook page, all signatories were also signing up to that.

'It's a little bit over-cautious, don't you think?' Ed said, when we met up at rehearsals later that night. Will, two years older than us – and in the spirit of the character, 'Uncle' Osbourne, whom he was playing – took a different view. 'If you want to design a pot to catch a lobster in, you don't tailor it so that it'll catch shrimp too. To every thing there is a purpose.' We youngsters saw his point.

Two days later Jack and Chris came up to us at breakfast and joined our table. It was the first time they'd done that. 'We were summoned to see the master last night,' Chris said. 'Those tapestries are quite something.'

'Did he give you a hard time?' Cocker asked.

'No, not really,' Chris said. 'Though we half expected it. He was keeping his powder dry, I think.'

'Yeah,' Jack said. 'It was more like he was just sounding us out. He wanted to know if we meant what we'd apparently said in the paper. That we'd happily move out of our room and into your two if it came to it. We said we stood by what we'd said. He's obviously aware of the petition, and that our two names are at the head of it.'

'And that was more or less that,' Chris said. 'He chatted a bit about our academic stuff, and then we left. His sherry's rather good.'

'Actually,' Jack came round to this point a bit shyly, 'we were wondering what your two rooms were like. It's just that…'

Neither Cocker nor I had given a thought to this. But now it was obvious. Chris and Jack had been wonderfully supportive, sticking their necks far out for us. But if the miracle happened and we went back to our old room and they went into ours … well, they'd be crossing their fingers that our two rooms would be all right.

With some trepidation we took them to see both our rooms immediately breakfast was finished. My bed wasn't made. The covers were all over the floor. It looked as if two energetic blokes had spent half the night fucking in it. That had been the case, of course. But we didn't need to tell them that. And they didn't need to ask.

They said they liked the rooms. Well, that was something. Even if they didn't mean it, it was good that they said that at least. We parted and said we'd all meet up again some time soon for a drink.

Later that day it was announced on Facebook that the petition was complete. All eight hundred and something undergrad and graduate members of the college had signed it. That included postal and email signatures from eight people who were away in France on a Geography field trip, two post-grad students who were researching Brazilian politics on the ground, one girl who was at home with her parents while recuperating from a bout of 'flu, and a guy who was in the John Radcliffe with something very unpleasant and gastric.

A copy of the petition was pinned up to the college notice-board outside the porter's lodge. Another – apparently, for Cocker and I were not in on this – was delivered to the master's office. Other copies (they each consisted of nine A4 pages) were sent to the bursar and – just in case – to the local press.

Then suddenly, the next day, it was all over. The master invited Cocker and me, and Jack and Chris, for another glass of his dry fino, fifteen minutes before dinner. He didn't ask us to sit down, but poured the sherry while we all stood. 'Your very good health, gentlemen,' he said, and we raised our glasses. He chewed his lips a bit then, like someone eating a stick of rhubarb, but after that he got his words out. 'I have to tell you, gentlemen, all four of you, that your campaign has been a success. You appear to have won a victory by recourse to democratic process. You may know that I have worked very close to the heart of democracy in Downing Street. Among the many things I learnt there was the fact that there are times in life – for all of us – when we have to bow to the inevitable with grace.' He took a graceful sip of sherry and the other four of us followed his lead. He resumed his speech. 'I can not on this occasion go against the unanimous will of the entire student body when it is expressed so clearly. The caveat, stated in the petition, that this is not to be taken as a precedent is very clear, and I'm reconnaissant of that. Gentlemen, you may exchange rooms tonight if you wish, though I would suggest that you leave it till tomorrow when there will be more time and daylight.'

He turned to Jack and Chris. 'I'm impressed by your willingness, as two very senior and respected members of this college, to support those younger than yourselves in a case that you clearly felt strongly about. An unselfish agenda like that counts in my book, and I have to admit that that has caused me to rethink. Gentlemen, please take a seat.' We all did, and so did the master. Then he addressed Jack and Chris again. 'I'm also impressed by your readiness to sacrifice your room in exchange for two smaller, first year ones. Perhaps next term it will be possible to move you into rooms more appropriate to your third-year status.' He turned to Cocker and me. 'I hope you'll appreciate that gesture of disinterested sacrifice.'

'I think we will,' Cocker said in a rather subdued voice.

To lighten the tone I raised my glass in the direction of the two older students. 'Thanks, guys,' I said. 'It's something we won't forget.' Then, to my surprise we all talked of general things for ten minutes while we finished our sherry. I suppose it was my imagination, or else the effect of a small current of air, but I did have the impression at one moment that one of the unicorns on one of the tapestries shook his mane and horn ever so slightly, and winked at us.

TWENTY

We all moved rooms in the morning. The porter lent us a barrow, which helped. But the stairs remained obdurately stairs for all of us, and by the time we'd finished we'd all worked up quite a sweat. It didn't matter. When the process was finished Cocker and I stood at last in the late morning silence in the room we'd shared in our first term. It wasn't in the old part of the college but in a building that had been put up in the second half of the twentieth century. The view from its window was of the bottom end of town, of the bus station, of Nuffield College and the Castle Mound. Not the pretty bit. That didn't matter in the least. It was our view. Our room. Our home. The room we'd fought for, and for which eight hundred people had campaigned on our behalf. We felt both proud and humble at the same time. We had come home.

Cocker said to me, 'You write the name card for the door. Both names in your hand-writing. And put your name first.' I was only too aware of the compliment he was paying me. In my clearest, finest capitals I wrote: *PIP ROGERS COCKER DAVIS*. These days it was nothing less than the truth. There was a little space at the bottom. Cocker took the pen from me and added, in smaller writing: *and Cocker rogers Pip.* He said, 'We might have to hide that if our parents come to visit, but it can stand for everybody else.'

For the next few days we just enjoyed spending time in our old room. If we had time away from lectures and tutorials together in the afternoons or even mornings, we'd spend it – not writing the essays for which there were deadlines – but simply lying together on one of our beds. Not having sex, not talking, sometimes not even stroking each other's hair. Just being where we wanted to be. Together. That was enough. And when bedtime did come round … well, the luxury of that, of not having to traipse through the college grounds to a different building, of not having to get up early and go back to our own room before the cleaning 'scouts' arrived… It was wonderful beyond belief.

Against that background the opening night of Journey's End stole up on us almost before we'd given it a thought. When it did come it was like the icing on the cake of our triumph. The show was packed out every night, Cocker and I were the undisputed stars of it, and it was because of our high profile that the house was packed night after night. Pride goeth before a fall, of course, and it might have been expected that after all the build up our performances would have been less than good, and disappointed people in their hundreds. But that didn't happen. Sometimes we get luckier than we deserve.

Whereas at the end of Hamlet I had died in Cocker's arms, at the end of Journey's End Cocker died in mine. Once again audiences were very moved by the scene, and so were Cocker and I. But we managed not to cry on stage this time round. Perhaps we were getting used to it. Getting used to the business of touching others' hearts. Perhaps we were learning to be actors. Perhaps we were growing up a bit.

Again the reviews in the newspapers were complimentary. Mick didn't write any of them this time round, explaining that he was now on much too close personal terms with some of the cast – though not going as far as telling his editors that in the case of one of them, Ed, those close personal terms included regular three-way sex. We appreciated those reviews all the more in the end for the fact that they were written by people we'd never met.

The following week it was our turn to sit in the audience for The Importance of Being Earnest: our turn to watch Giles and Mick delivering some of Wilde's most burnished one-liners. And two-liners and ten-liners. You have to hand it to the guy sometimes. We went on the opening night because there was going to be a bit of a party afterwards and we'd been invited to it. The show was on at the North Wall centre, which meant a bit of a hike up into North Oxford – a place inhabited mainly by dons and other people who owned cars – but we were promised a lift back.

They were a pretty good double act, Giles and Mick, as Jack and Algernon. And the woman who played Lady Bracknell was also good. She was the director's wife. The other players weren't quite so strong, but who were we to nit-pick? We were only amateurs ourselves, after all, and we'd been given free tickets.

Afterwards there were drinks at the bar, and Giles introduced Cocker and me – and Ed and Will, who had also been invited – to the rest of the cast. Some people began to drift off. They included the director and his wife. As the numbers thinned it became easier to realise who was coming to the party, which was to be held at Giles's house. It was also beginning to look like the party was male only, and I drew a rather obvious inference from that.

Cocker and I were driven back to Jericho by a youngish guy who had aged up, with the help of make-up and powder in the hair, to play Canon Chasuble. Ed and Will were given a lift by someone else. The Chasuble guy, whose name was Jason, made it clear to us in the car that he knew exactly who we were. He'd seen us in Journey's End, also in Hamlet. 'I have to congratulate you, though,' he said as he threaded through the night-time streets, 'on getting your room back. That was a terrific campaign you had with Mick.'

'We're very lucky to have Mick as a friend,' Cocker said.

'He's a great guy,' Jason said. He gave a little laugh. 'And very lovely in bed. Though I expect you already know that.'

'Actually we don't,' said Cocker very quickly and a bit primly. I think he was afraid that if I'd spoken I'd have given away the fact that I had actually been in Giles's bed. Though I guessed that all Giles's friends probably knew that anyway.

We arrived and parked – which wasn't easy – and then walked to the door of Giles's house. Jason led the way in, and presented Cocker and me with great pride, as if he'd just landed us with a fishing net.

I'd wondered in advance if at this sort of party – a party for twenty-somethings and thirty-year-olds – the thing would be carried forward by cocaine snorts or amphetamines or things I hadn't even heard of. But it wasn't. It was carried forward by those two good old pall-bearers, alcohol and sex.

I don't know if the Dry Martini had been invented when The Importance was premiered in 1895. I think perhaps it only came in during Prohibition in the States in the 1920s or whenever it was. But anyway, Martini cocktails were the drink of this night. They came shaken not stirred, as J. Bond would have insisted, in large glasses half full of ice. An olive – no pansy lemon twist – adorned the mix, and the rest, as Shakespeare might have said, at the risk of puncturing his metre, was gin. And a little bit of Martini Seco floated in on top.

Reader, you know what a Martini cocktail is. You know its effects. You may well know the effect of two of them. Or three. Cocker and I did not. As learning curves went, this one was steep.

It became difficult to judge where Cocker was in the room and where I was. I wasn't sure from moment to moment whether remarks addressed to me were meant also for both of us. When arms came round me, was that embrace meant to include Cocker too? I hoped it was each time, but couldn't be sure. My peripheral vision seemed to have taken a comfort break.

I realised after a while that everyone except me seemed to have taken their cock out. Some were flaccid, some fully erect. As everyone is who confronts this spectacle for the first time, I was struck by the infinite variety that nature has conjured in her aeon-old attack on sameness. There were long thin ones, short fat ones, some with knobs on, others with tasselled hoods...

Through a haze Cocker swam up to me as if in a murky fish tank. His dick was not on show, and I was glad of that. He said, in a voice of such timid uncertainty that it hurt, 'I'd like to go home now. If that's what you would like.'

I realised then that there was nothing more in the world that I'd like. There was nothing more in the world I'd have ever liked.

We couldn't put into words how bruised we both were at that moment. We certainly couldn't have explained why. We left the party without saying goodnight or thank you to anyone. We didn't care. We only wanted to be us.

The cold night air of March in Oxford knocked us about as we walked back from Jericho along Walton Street. Occasionally we lurched into each other. Cocker said, 'Sorry. I didn't mean to bully you. Would you have liked to stay?'

'For a moment, yes,' I admitted. 'But not for longer than that.' I had to think for a second about what I wanted to say next. I said it. It came out a bit starkly. 'I don't put up with being bullied. Not normally. But from you it doesn't count.'

I learnt another lesson about love at that moment. Falling in love with another person is like combing your hair. It's not something you do just the once.

There was a bit of a problem when we got into bed. The room wouldn't stay put. We had to get out and sit on the edge of the bed for twenty minutes in order to avoid being sick. And when we got back in there was no question of any sort of sex. Even so, it was nice. It was good to be in the right place.

Now that Journey's End was finished there was no particular reason why we should meet up again with either Will or Ed. But Oxford is not an enormous city and you were always running into people in the street. Two days after the party, and one day after our hangovers had worn off, I met Will in Sainsbury's in Magdalen Street. That wouldn't have been significant in itself. What made it so was that he wasn't alone. He was with Ed.

'Oh hi,' I said. 'Good to see you both.'

Ed answered. 'Good to *be* us both.'

'I see,' I said. 'I'm not sure there's an answer to that. Except that if it means what I think it means… Well, I think that's great.'

Will was smiling quietly. He let Ed answer. 'It's a bit of a bummer being in different colleges. Reckon you can use your skills to get us a double room somewhere?'

'That might be beyond even my powers,' I said.

A week later the four of us met up for a drink. It was good to see Will and Ed still together. Who would have thought that something that looked like surviving at least till the end of term could come out of an evening of Martini cocktails and group sex?

The end of term. Suddenly it was upon us. Cocker and I were not going to be separated this time. Over

Christmas it had hurt too much. We'd told our parents we would spend the first half of the vac with mine on Exmoor and the second half with his in Tunbridge Wells.

We travelled together by train. The countryside still lay under the spell of winter. The two hundred and more miles of it we travelled were still asleep. It was hard to believe that when we returned to Oxford in a few weeks' time it would all be greening up.

My mother met us at Exeter St David's. I had difficulty putting away the hard memory of the last time we'd met face to face. At this very station, when I'd wrenched myself away from her grasp. She was remembering the moment too, I realised. I could see that from the look on her face. But a lot had happened in the meantime. Our phone-calls and letters had gone some way towards healing that wound in our relationship. There would be a scar, of course. Neither of us would ever really forget it. But that is life.

Arriving at the house in Oare I wondered which room Cocker and I would be given. If Mum had prepared one of the guest rooms for us, the one with the double bed, one very clear message would be given. But she hadn't done that. She'd made up the two single beds in my own room, where we'd slept last time. Back then she hadn't known about Cocker and me. Now she did. So what message was I to take from that signal? One room but two beds. I talked about this with Cocker as we unpacked.

'I think it's that thing about people knowing but not wanting to know too much,' he said. 'I think we'll find, when we get to Tunbridge Wells, my parents are much the same about that.'

'Like they're saying they know we have sex together but don't want to think about it?' I said.

'Yeah,' he said. 'I think it means they expect us to get into one bed together and make love as per normal but be quiet about it.'

'That's what we'll do, then,' I said, nodding sagely. Then we interrupted our unpacking for a moment to give each other a hug and kiss.

In the evening we met up with Alex in The Rising Sun at Lynmouth. Cocker, uninsured, and without my mother's knowledge, drove her car down Countisbury Hill without any show of trepidation and with my hand gently cupping the mound in his denim-clad crotch.

Alex was still with Kieran and, I could tell from Alex's face, still very much in love. However, Kieran wasn't actually with us this evening. Alex would be joining him in Exeter tomorrow. Cocker asked Alex if their parents knew about them yet. They hadn't been *told* yet, was Alex's lawyerly response.

'Actually, neither have mine,' said Cocker. Out of all of us it seemed I was the only one who had crossed that particular Rubicon. If my experience was anything to go by it wasn't going to be as easy for the others as all that.

TWENTY-ONE

Reading signs and omens into things, especially negative ones… I'd been trying to grow out of that. But I had a presentiment about things when we had that conversation. About the fact that neither Alex nor Kieran nor Cocker had come out to their parents. Sometimes you have a presentiment and nothing happens. Sometimes it all comes to pass horribly at once.

I had a call from Alex the next afternoon. Cocker and I were idling the time away watching a DVD. We were supposed to be meeting Alex and Kieran in the evening. I was shocked to hear the distress in Alex's voice. 'They've kicked us out. Kieran's parents have. They said, yes, we're adults and can do what we want, but please would we not do it in their house. Kieran's so upset he can't speak. We're driving to my folks' place, but I don't know…'

I cut him off. 'Where are you?'

'Crossing Exmoor. Near Simonsbath…'

'Don't go home straight away,' I said. 'Don't let Kieran have to deal with your parents. Talk to us first.'

'Yeah, but…'

'Be at The Rising Sun in half an hour. We'll be there first.'

I relayed all this to Cocker. 'Oh shit,' he said.

I told my mother we were going out earlier than we'd arranged, and not to expect us for dinner. We'd get something to eat somewhere while we were out. 'Make sure you do,' she said. 'And drive carefully.'

It was raining hard, and the afternoon had gone dark. It got darker as we approached the one in four descent of Countisbury cliff. Cocker wasn't driving this time. I was. The rain lashed the road surface as we descended, headlights cutting into the gloom before us. Brakes and steering didn't seem to do much on a surface suddenly as slippery as glass. I set my course straight down the hill and held the steering-wheel with grim fastness. Cocker's hand saucered my crotch, and I was grateful for that. He didn't undo my fly, though. He knew how hard I needed to concentrate.

We reached the bottom with great relief, and coasted round the bends, across the River Lyn, and parked outside the pub. Through the sheeting rain we ran inside.

We had arrived first. We bought ourselves a pint of Badger each and sat in the cosiness of the bar, looking out at the wild weather we had just escaped.

There is something very comforting about being in this position: of looking out from a place of warmth and safety at other people confronting a dangerous situation you've just come through unscathed. From our snug table we had a view through the small-paned window of the Countisbury climb. In orderly fashion a line of red lights rose like ascending aircraft, while close alongside pairs of white headlights on low-beam came cautiously down through the teeming black and silver rain.

Then, 'Oh God!' said Cocker. A pair of headlights detached themselves from the patient descending line. They slid across the road, slicing the climbing dotted line of red. The red intensified as scores of brake-lights came quickly on. The headlights were out on their own now. Free of the two lines, the white and red, they seemed to hover in the darkness for an instant. And then they fell.

When you strike a match and flick it out across a dark stream and it falls and goes out… When you look at Blake's painting of The Fall of Lucifer… But it was worse than that. Real people were in that fall into eternity. Worse even than that. I knew with a terrible certainty that I'd witnessed the dying moments of Kieran and my oldest friend.

I yelled at Cocker, 'We got to get there.' We ran out of the pub and into the lashing rain and dark. There was no point, no point at all. It had all happened half a mile away. We'd never get there. There'd be nothing we could do even if we did.

We crossed the road at a sprint, darting between the traffic, and ran down onto the rocky beach. A terrible noise had started up amidst the crashing of the rain. A kind of howling. I couldn't think where it was coming from at first. Then I realised it was coming from my throat.

For twenty minutes we scrambled over rocks in the slippery dark. Then there were lights ahead. Flashing lights above us told us the police and ambulance services had arrived. A helicopter came and buzzed overhead. A string of lights was descending the cliff. A policeman appeared in front of us. God knew how he'd got down here. 'Gentlemen, I'm sorry,' he said. 'You can't go any further. There's been an accident.'

'We know that, fuck you,' said Cocker, more angry than I'd ever heard him. 'We've just lost our two best mates.'

'How do you know that?' said the policeman calmly.

'We just know it,' I said.

The policeman spread himself like a net in front of us to stop us moving forwards. He placed a gloved hand on the shoulder of each of us. 'I'm sorry, kids,' he said.

The days that followed were as unreal as nightmares, but far worse. For everything that happened was real; there was nothing from which we could ever be released; no dawn awakening could be looked forward to that would unpick the fabric of it.

I can't tell you how we spent those days. I've tried to bury my memories of them. There were people to speak to; there were two funerals to attend. Alex's parents didn't go to Kieran's funeral, Kieran's didn't go to Alex's. Cocker and I were the only two people who attended both.

The day after the second one – it was Alex's – we travelled to Tunbridge Wells. It was something to do. A way of escaping the Exmoor awfulness. But it was a long journey. If England was the face of a clock that was saying twenty to six, then Exmoor was at the end of the big hand, and Tunbridge Wells at the end of the short one, after you'd passed through London at the hub. It rained throughout.

Cocker's parents seemed unsure about how to handle us. We were both still in shock. Our arrival together in the wake of the death of two gay friends who were a couple … well, it was hardly the easiest way for Cocker to come out. Cocker was given his usual bedroom, I was given a small spare room one floor above. It wasn't what Cocker had expected and certainly not what either of us wanted, but we were too cowed and traumatised by what had happened to put up any kind of fight.

I resigned myself to sleeping alone that first night. At least Cocker and I were in the same house. At least neither of us was dead.

I was woken by the door opening: by the widening crack of light. It was Cocker in a dressing-gown. I'd never seen that dressing-gown before. It was the one he used … I nearly wrote *at home.* I meant, in Tunbridge Wells.

He came towards my bed. I sat bolt upright. He said to me in a voice that trembled, through teeth that chattered, 'I'm ill. I'm scared. I don't know what I've got…'

'Just get into bed with me,' I said. I threw the duvet back and he got in with me, then I pulled the duvet up again and wrapped us both in it.

As I've said, Cocker's father was a doctor. By five o'clock in the morning, when the treatment I'd tried on Cocker – wrapping him in my arms and in my love, which had worked so well when he'd had a chill at Oxford half a year ago – had failed to work this time, I went to his parents' room and woke them up. Cocker hadn't slept. He had a headache that was becoming agonising and a painfully stiff neck.

Cocker's father didn't bother to dress. He put a coat on over his pyjamas and drove Cocker in his dressing-gown, and me in another one his father threw at me, directly to Pembury A and E. Even dressed as he was Cocker's father was recognised, and the gravity of the situation too. They waved us through to triage and at that point I was relegated to the ranks of those who sit and wait outside while Cocker and his father went in.

It was meningitis. It was caused by all kinds of things. Living with other people was one of them. It could be triggered by stress. Cocker's father told me all about it as he drove me back to his house in the early morning. I'd hardly met the man. But I knew he was scared that his son might die. I was scared my lover might die. They were the two most awful things that either of us could imagine happening to us, and yet neither of us could say this to the other. I don't know if this was a lesson about love, or about something else.

It didn't get better that day. Cocker was in intensive care. Only his parents were allowed to visit. They might have made an exception for me if they'd known me better, but they didn't think to do that. Grief does blind you to the needs of others. Instead, Cocker's mother said to me, 'Please don't take this the wrong way but I don't think you can help your friend by being here right now. Be strong for him in your own way and you'll see him ever so soon, God willing, back at Oxford.' It was a very pretty speech, and I had to make allowance for the fact that it was made by a mother whose feelings were on the rack … but I couldn't mistake its meaning. It meant get out.

I couldn't go back to Somerset. I was beyond dealing with my parents. I phoned Giles. I got on the train to London, and from there I took another one, on the familiar line from Paddington to Oxford.

The willows at least were coming into leaf. Death comes to us all but in March of every year the willows along the loops of the Thames will still come into leaf. Hoping against hope I texted Cocker hourly, but no answer came.

I arrived at Giles's front door after wheeling my luggage for a mile and a half. I knocked. He opened the door. 'Come in, little angel,' he said.

We had to get one thing out of the way that evening as we sipped our Jack Daniel's. I said, 'I hope you won't mind if I don't sleep with you.'

Giles put his handsome head on one side. 'Won't mind is an odd way of putting it. I'll always want to… but I'll agree that we won't. You want to wait for Cocker. And he'll be back before you can say knife.'

'I wish I could be so sure,' I said. 'He might die…'

'He won't,' Giles said.

We were sitting on opposite sofas. Mick wasn't in yet, so there were just the two of us. I said, 'Can I come and sit next to you?'

'If that's what you want,' Giles said.

I walked across to him and sat right next to him, the way I'd done the night we'd first met. 'Put your arm around me, please,' I said. He did. Then I laid my head upon his chest. I listened to the beating of his heart.

I spent my days writing this. Writing what you've just been reading. It's been much quicker for you to read it than it was for me to write. I texted Cocker daily but nothing came back. Tried to phone. No response. I didn't try to contact his parents. If there was bad news no doubt I'd hear it in due course.

The vacation ended. Trundling my suitcase out of Jericho and along Walton Street I moved back into college, into the room that was mine and Cocker's. Though now it was mine alone. I had a spare bed in it. I could have invited anybody I might want. I wanted nobody, of course, except... well, I don't have to spell it out. It was all spelled out on the door. Pip rogers Cocker Davis and Cocker rogers Pip. I didn't know if that would ever be true again, or whether it would have to be put, at some point, into the past tense. For the moment I left the message proudly in place.

I didn't want to see people. I didn't want my friends. The more sympathetic they were the more everything hurt. James was going to direct a play. He wanted me in it. I didn't want to hear about it.

One lovely thing happened. It was something Giles said when we met in the Morse bar one night. 'Know what? Actually, except for Ed and Will, you're the first person we've told. Mick and I are going for a civil partnership. We think we want to be just the two of us from now on. Especially since Will and Ed...' Giles broke off and stared into his expensive drink. 'Actually, it was you and Cocker who set us the example in that.'

It was, I thought. Past tense. I had another of my terrible presentiments. That slip of the tenses on Giles's part... That was the bell that tolled for Cocker. This was the moment – it was twenty minutes past nine this

Tuesday night – of Cocker's death. I'd hear soon enough. By email. By phone. Or by text.

I stood up. 'Sorry, Giles,' I said. 'But d'you mind if I love you and leave you right now? Catch up tomorrow perhaps.'

Giles looked up at me. *Fondly* described the way he did that. 'Are you sure you're all right on your own, little angel?' he said.

'I'll be fine, and I'm not on my own,' I said.

'OK then,' said Giles. 'But if you're not OK…' He picked up his phone and tapped it.

'Received and understood,' I said. Then I turned and walked out into the dark.

I turned right as I left The Randolph. Right again into Magdalen Street and down to Carfax. I went on into Cornmarket Street, and then continued down St Aldates past Christchurch towards the river. The Head of the River was brightly lit and looked busy. I thought about going in, but I hadn't gone into a pub on my own since … well, since all of that.

Instead I went out onto the bridge – Folly Bridge: I still didn't know why it was called that – and stood there, listening to the water cascading over the weir below me, seeing its foam as dim white streaks in the dark.

I thought I'd dealt with the issue of homesickness when I'd gone away to boarding school all those years before. Thought I'd worked my way through it in my early years there. Thought it couldn't come back to haunt me, hurt me, ever again. At this moment I discovered that was not the case. The city around me was beautiful in the extreme, I gave it that. But it was alien to me. Whatever the opposite of home was, this was it.

I felt rather than saw that someone had come up and was standing beside me, leaning, as I was, over the parapet of the bridge. A voice I recognised asked me, 'Are you all right?'

I turned in wonder and astonishment. It was Cocker.

'Oh fuck,' I said. 'How…?'

'Tell you later,' he said.

He took me in his arms and kissed me. I started crying then. Cocker stroked my hair till I heard the crackle of it. 'Let's go home,' he said.

EPILOGUE

It's mid-summer in Oxford. Cocker and I have been punting on the river, drifting along under the trees. We've walked together, sometimes with other friends – with Giles and Mick, or with Will and Ed – along the Thames Path to The Trout at Godstow. In the summer the walk is glorious, as the path tunnels beneath over-arching hawthorn branches that are white with May flowers, and water flows past on either side. It opens out into meadows grazed by friendly cows and steers. The bare ruined choir of Godstow priory is full of sun and birdsong, and the pub, when you reach it, gives you a view of the river from the terrace, that is overhung by chestnut and beech trees. The countryside invades Oxford, and Oxford reaches out into the countryside.

Exams are over. We are doing The Tempest in the college gardens, beside the lake. I am playing Prospero. Cocker, cast against type this time, is a rather butch Ariel. We don't die in each other's arms in this one. We're not too worried about that. We spend about eight hours in every twenty-four in that place of security and warmth. We have done so now for nearly three years.

For this is not our first summer at Oxford but our third. We have become one of the institutions of the place. The best-known gay couple in the university. Yet within a few days we shall be out of it, leaving the safe reaches of its stream for the ocean that is the life that follows. About that there is much that is uncertain. We've been offered auditions for a professional theatre company, both of us. Don't know if we'll get them: it's a tough world out there.

Things we do know, though: we're having our civil partnership ceremony next week. We've stayed the course till now. And nothing will shake us apart after that. Cocker and I together till Kingdom come, even when Oxford, or at least our memories of it, have faded like a dream. Together till the day that death parts us…

And now, as my cue comes to ascend the makeshift stage among the trees through which the lake winks in the light of the evening lamps, I realise how strange and powerful this moment of impending departure is. It's all there in the lines of Prospero I am about to speak.

I'm on stage now. I hold up my hand. The audience, seated in chairs upon the grass, is pin-drop quiet. Cocker will not appear, as Ariel, until another minute has passed. But I can see him awaiting his cue in the shadows beneath the trees. It is of him that I think as I open my mouth and those words of Shakespeare's – greater words than any of mine – come out…

Be cheerful, sir:
Our revels now are ended. These our actors,
As I foretold you, were all spirits and
Are melted into air, into thin air:
And like the baseless fabric of this vision…

With an expansive gesture I indicate the floodlit buildings behind me, the Georgian, the medieval wings of the college, the dreaming spires beyond…

The cloud-capped towers, the gorgeous palaces,

The solemn temples, the great globe itself,
Yea, all which it inherit…

Here I sweep my hand gravely across my view of the audience.

… shall dissolve
And, like this insubstantial pageant faded,
Leave not a rack behind. We are such stuff
As dreams are made on…

I risk a look at Cocker at this point. He waits in the half-shadow, looking more wonderful than I've ever seen him in these three years. He is looking up, and his eyes are full of me.

…and our little life
Is rounded with a sleep.

THE END

****

Anthony McDonald is the author of more than twenty novels. He studied modern history at Durham University, then worked briefly as a musical instrument maker and as a farmhand before moving into the theatre, where he has worked in every capacity except director and electrician. He has also spent several years teaching English in Paris and London. He now lives in rural East Sussex, England.

Novels by Anthony McDonald

Gay Romance Series:
Sweet Nineteen
Gay Romance on Garda
Gay Romance in Majorca
The Paris Novel
Cocker and I
Cam Cox
The Van Gogh Window
Gay Romance in Tartan
Tibidabo
Spring Sonata
Touching Fifty
Romance on the Orient Express

Also:

SILVER CITY
IVOR'S GHOSTS
ADAM
BLUE SKY ADAM
GETTING ORLANDO
ORANGE BITTER, ORANGE SWEET
ALONG THE STARS
WOODCOCK FLIGHT

Anthony McDonald

RALPH: DIARY OF A GAY TEEN
THE DOG IN THE CHAPEL
TOM AND CHRISTOPHER AND THEIR KIND
DOG ROSES
MATCHES IN THE DARK:
13 Tales of Gay Men
(Short story collection)

All titles are available as Kindle ebooks and as
paperbacks from Amazon.
www.anthonymcdonald.co.uk

30745977R00107

Printed in Great Britain
by Amazon